佛夢達
FORMONDA

可愛怡家族的命運

王克謙、王凱琳／合著

獻給

我在台灣的爺爺奶奶

和

我在英國的爺爺奶奶

目錄

序幕 Who-You-You-Who

　　當艾迪亞聽到一個奇怪的聲音時，她正坐在她最喜歡的長板凳上看書。天空的顏色突然變暗。

　　戰爭要開始了，這是第二次世界大戰。艾迪亞是住在德國的一個少女，她在班上成績數一數二。她知道世界上每個角落發生的事情，因為她看許多的新聞。她知道納粹正在侵略許多其他國家。

　　想都別想！愚蠢的德國人！她想。你應該要做的是和盟軍合作。

　　炸彈的聲音突然在每個人的耳邊爆響開來，此時教堂鐘塔的鐘也剛好敲響了五下。

　　喔喔！快要晚餐時間了，我最好趕快回家。

　　艾迪亞跑回家的途中，英軍的炸彈像雨點一樣落下。公園裡開始著火，樹木頓時燃起熊熊火焰，人們忙著抱起他們的小孩逃竄。

　　我都已經十五歲了，還是覺得那些小嬰孩看起來很惹人厭……嗯！

Prologue Who-You-You-Who

Adiale was sitting on a bench when she heard a strange sound. The sky went dark.

A war began, it was World War II. As a teenage girl in Germany, Adiale was top of her class. She knew what was happening in every corner of the world because she watched too much news. She knew about the Nazi's invasion.

Don't overthink it, you stupid Germans! You should be their allies! Adiale thought.

The sound of bombing started to explode in everyone's ears. Then, the bell in the tower rang five times.

Uh oh! It's almost dinner, I'd better get home.

She ran home as English bombs started falling and set the park on fire. The trees burst up in flames, people ran to get their babies and children.

I am a mature 15 year old and I still think the sight of babies are disgusting. Urgh!

當她正在這樣想時，突然看見一個老人，在周遭一片慌亂之中，安然地坐在一個長椅上閉目打坐。他至少有七、八十歲了，有著滿頭的白髮和很長的白鬍鬚。突然，一陣強風吹過，那個老人不見了！

大概是我的眼睛有毛病吧！艾迪亞眨眨眼，繼續往回家的路上奔跑。

第二天，艾迪亞迫不及待地跑去公園，要看看那個她最喜歡坐在上面看書的長板凳是否依然無恙。雖然別人都覺得她的想法很蠢，因為公園已經被摧毀了，但是，看！它還好好地在那裡！

「Who-You-You-Who。」一個聲音突然出現。

艾迪亞感到背脊一陣發涼。她轉頭撇見一隻枯瘦的手放在她的肩上，一個老人的臉正對著她微微地笑著。

「呀！」艾迪亞大叫一聲，「是你！那個打坐的老人！」

「是的，噓……小聲一點。來，跟我來。」

「我不能跟你走。」

「我知道妳不能，但是妳必須。」

「好吧！」

But then, she saw in the midst of all the confusion, a man sitting on a bench, meditating. He had to at least be 70 or 80 years old. He had a long white beard with lots of white hair. When a gust of wind came by, the man disappeared!

It must have just been me. Adiale blinked her eyes, then raced home for dinner.

The next day, Adiale went to see if her favorite reading spot was available. Most people would call her dumb, but she wasn't. When she got there, the bench was in one piece!

"Who-You-You-Who," a voice said.

A tickle ran along her spine. She turned her head to find a bony hand laid on her shoulder and an old person's face gently smiling at her.

"Aah!" Adiale yelled. "It's you! The meditating guy!"

"That's right. Shh…, you have to be quiet. Here, come with me."

"But I can't!"

"I know you can't, but you have to!"

"Fine!"

第一章　## 跳越區

「所以，你叫什麼名字？」艾迪亞問。

「我姓藍普提，」老人回答，「戴天尼·藍普提。走吧！別浪費時間。」

他們動身，沿著小樹林旁的一條河邊一直走，走了許久。樹木的形狀開始變得奇怪，天空的顏色變成紫色。艾迪亞意識到他們已經置身在一個不一樣的世界裡。

「我們在哪裡？」艾迪亞問。她可以看到在他們前進的方向不遠處有一些建築物。

「噓……在這裡要盡量放低聲音，要不然你就會自找麻煩。這是一個跳越區，叫做周尼波町。它被一個很邪惡的人統治，我告訴妳，他的名字做強柯。」

「等等！你說**這一個**跳越區，所以，還有很多其他跳越區？」

「是的。一個跳越區在佛夢達的世界裡就像是一個省分一樣。」

「佛夢達？」

Chapter I **Jumpers**

"So, what's your name?" Adiale asked.

"Lamputi," the old man said. "Derteinium Lamputi. Let's go! No hesitation."

So they left the park and walked beside a river next to a grove. The trees started to change into a weird shape and the color of the sky was becoming more purple. Adiale soon realized they were in a new world.

"Where are we now?" Adiale asked. She could see some buildings in the distance, in the direction that they were approaching.

"Hush, try to keep low profile here or you will put yourself in big trouble! This is a Jumper called Juniperdinto. It is ruled by an evil man. Let me tell you, his name is Jrunk Lerwan."

"Wait, did you say THIS Jumper? So there are more?" Adiale asked.

"Yes. A Jumper is like a province in the world of Formonda."

"Formonda?"

「對了，你的全名是什麼？」

「艾迪亞・珍妮・海根。」

「好，艾迪亞・珍妮・海根，因為妳在佛夢達背負了一個很重要的任務，在我們碰到危險之前，我必須先教妳一個特別的法力。」

老人戴天尼於是開始示範一些奇怪的手勢。

「不要用——」老人戴天尼還沒來得及把話說完，艾迪亞已經照做。她的雙手捧起來，然後往外甩出去。她的眼睛變成黃色，一陣旋風電漿從她的雙手噴射出來。她突然往上飛起，浮在空中。她所可以看到腳底下的東西，除了老人戴天尼之外，都開始扭曲變形，並捲起來，最終消失，像是被黑洞吸進去了一樣。

「老天！被解決掉了……」老人戴天尼一邊說一邊往後退。

「這一招叫做爾卓式，是一種傳奇性的法力。它可以導致整個跳越區的存在被完全撤回、抵銷掉。」老人戴天尼解釋。

「下一次，請妳小心一點！只有當你真的需要的時候才用它。」他嘆了一口氣。「來吧，是時候上路，開始我們的冒險了。」

"Anyway, what's your full name?" asked Derteinium.

"Adiale Juniphèr Hagën."

"Ok, Adiale Juniphèr Hagën, because you carry a very important mission here in Formonda, I need to teach you a special power before we run into any danger."

Then Derteinium started showing Adiale a move using his hands.

"Do NOT use —" Just before Derteinium could finish his sentence, Adiale had tried to mimic the move by cupping her hands and throwing them out in the air. Her eyes turned to yellow, then a plasma was ejected from her hands. Adiale suddenly flew up and was floating in the air. Things that she could see, except for Derteinium, started to twist and roll, then finally disappeared, like being sucked into a black hole.

Adiale just destroyed everything in this Jumper, by accident.

"Oh, my! That settles it…," said Derteinium while stepping back.

"That was called the 'Adro', a legendary power to undo the existence of a Jumper," Derteinium explained.

"Next time, be careful, please! Only use it when you have to," he sighed. "Now, it's time for our adventure."

他們動身起行。沒多久，他們看到三個男孩。其中一個，有著咖啡色的頭髮，髮型很奇特，一撮一撮往上刺，背著一個雙肩背包。他跟艾迪亞打招呼：

「嗨！你好！」

「嗯……嗨？」艾迪亞回應。

「我看得出來妳是從地球來的。我跟妳一樣，也是從地球來的。」那個男孩繼續說：「我的名字叫克喜。我有幾個朋友介紹給妳認識。這個是阿米，另外這個是真要昇。我們都是從地球的同一個時間來的，我們來自 2017 年。你是從哪一年來的？」

「1939 年。」艾迪亞回答。

「是喔！ 我還有另外兩個朋友是從地球來的，蝦肉是從 1956 年來的，他是日本人。將安是從 1972 年來的，他是美國人。 」

「妳身邊這個人是誰？」阿米問艾迪亞。

They set off. Soon enough on their way, they saw three boys. One of them, with coffee-brown colored spiky hair and carrying a backpack, greeted them,

"Hi!"

"Eh, Hi…?" Adiale responded.

"I can tell that you are from Earth. I'm from Earth, too," the boy said. "My name is Chrishie. I have a few friends that I want you to meet. This is Armi, and this is TruEthan. We all came from the same time of Earth. We are from the year of 2017. Which year are you from?"

"1939," Adiale responded.

"I see. There are another two boys from Earth. Sharo is from 1956, he is Japanese. John is from 1972. He is American."

"Who is this person standing next to you?" Armi asked Adiale.

「你應該要記得我的！」老人戴天尼說。「我就是發明可以來到佛夢達的『邀請通道』的人！」

「喔！戴天尼・藍普提！」阿米拍著自己的臉。

真要昇突然插話進來。「嗨！我是真要昇。阿米和我都是克喜的好朋友。」 真要昇說道。「克喜，我們應該要走了，天快黑了！」

「好，我們繼續走吧！」克喜說著，從他的背包裡拿出幾個裝置出來。他把一個平板電腦連結上一個長相奇怪的機器。艾迪亞指著那些機器，說：

「那是什麼？」

「這就是讓我們可以開始這一切的東西！」克喜有點不耐煩。

他按下一個按鈕，前方馬上出現了一個漩渦入口，把他們全部都吸進去了。他們在一個像蟲洞一樣的空間裡穿梭，正在前往另一個不同的跳越區。此時艾迪亞突然想起一個問題。

「等等，我是怎麼來到這裡的？」艾迪亞問老人戴天尼。

「Who-You-You-Who。」老人回答她。

「Who-You……什麼？什麼？」艾迪亞問說。

"You should remember me!" Derteinium said, "I'm the one who built the Invite Tunnel for entering Formonda."

"Oh, Derteinium Lamputi!" Armi facepalmed.

TruEthan came in that instant. "Hi, I am TruEthan. Armi and I are Chrishie's best friends." TruEthan said. "Chrishie, we should get going. It's getting dark."

"Okay. Let's get a move on!" Chrishie took out a few devices from his backpack, then connected a tablet computer to a weird machine. Adiale pointed at the device and asked,

"What is that?"

"The thing that started this whole thing!" Chrishie said impatiently.

He pressed a button, a portal appeared and sucked them in. Now they were travelling in a wormhole, off to a new Jumper. Adiale suddenly thought about something.

"Wait, so how did I get here in the first place?" Adiale asked Derteinium.

"Who-You-You-Who," Derteinium responded.

"Who-You-What-What?" Adiale asked.

「Who-You-You-Who，這是一個能夠進入『邀請通道』的咒語。」老人戴天尼說。

「你是怎麼來到這裡的？」艾迪亞轉頭問克喜。

「我？喔，這個世界是被我創造出來的！用神祕的大十魔法。」

「嗯……什麼是大十魔法？」

克喜很驚訝，「妳不知道什麼是大十魔法？這從 1999 年開始就有了！喔，我忘了妳是從 1939 年來的了。」

「嗶嗶嗶嗶……」那個機器傳出了響聲。

「我們到了！」克喜說。前方出現了一個門口。

他們走出去，眾人驚訝得鴉雀無聲。

"Who-You-You-Who. It's the magic word to travel through the Invite Tunnel," Derteinium answered.

"How did you end up here?" Adiale turned to ask Chrishie.

"Me? Oh, I was the one who created this world, with the deep magic of Dash."

"Eh…, what is Dash?"

Chrishie seemed surprised, "You don't know what Dash is? It has been since 1999! Oh yeah, I forgot you are from 1939."

"Beeeeeeep!" the machine sounded.

"Oh, we're here," Chrishie said.

A portal opened and there was stunned silence.

第二章　　波理斯瑪

「歡迎來到波理斯瑪！」克喜說，「我們的下一站是
樂凡第。」

「何必再去其他的跳越區？！這一個多好！太完美
了！」真要昇高興地說。

「喔，因為我知道這一個跳越區很快就要結束了。」
克喜的回答很令人掃興。

這一個跳越區，波理斯瑪，是一個迷人的大花園，充
滿了五顏六色的各式花朵。周圍的海水反射著陽光，波光
粼粼。有幾個飛龍快樂地在野草上玩噴火的遊戲。到處都
有橘紅色的火焰，這裡一簇，那裡一簇，讓這一個跳越區
的設計看來特別與眾不同。

在東邊有一個宮殿，是用玻璃、水晶、和石英做成
的，在陽光底下閃閃發亮。這個宮殿是屬於這個跳越區的
統治者，卡爾王子的。他是一個英俊的年輕人，也是一個
獵人。這個美麗的宮殿同時也是一個漂亮的女孩，若薇亞
公主的住所。她是卡爾王子的妹妹。

Chapter II **Purisima**

"Welcome to Purisima!" Chrishie said, "Our next stop will be La Frontier."

"Why are we going to another Jumper?" TruEthan asked, "This one is perfect!"

"Oh, I know for a fact that this one will end very soon." Chrishie just ruined everyone's day with what he said.

This Jumper, Purisima, had beautiful gardens with seas of reflected sunlight and happy dragons breathing fire on weeds. The orangish fires blazed up here and there, making the sight of this Jumper so amazing.

In the east, a palace made of glass, crystal, and quartz shimmered in the sunlight. It was the palace of the ruler, Prince Kale. He was a handsome young man, also a great hunter. This beautiful palace was also the residence of a beautiful girl, Princess Rovia. She was Prince Kale's sister.

　　若薇亞公主身上散發出一種金色的光芒，她有一頭藍色的頭髮，當被風吹起的時候，就像水一樣柔軟流暢。她和善、輕巧、熱切，在波理斯瑪的每個人都喜歡她。可惜啊！這個年輕女孩子的心裡卻有一個沒有人知道的煩惱。

　　眞要昇在第一眼就愛上了若薇亞公主。

　　「歡迎來到波理斯瑪！我是若薇亞公主。」

　　「很漂……很好……我叫眞要昇。」

　　「我希望你們會喜歡波理斯瑪，我的家園。」

　　「這是一個很壯觀的地方！其他的跳越區根本不能比！」

　　「是嗎？我從來沒有去過其他的跳越區。」若薇亞公主看著遠方，眼裡有一絲絲的傷感。「我從來沒有離開過波理斯瑪。」

　　他倆之間的對話就是這樣開始的。第二天眞要昇又回來找若薇亞公主，後天，大後天，每一天都這樣。他們會一邊走一邊聊天，主要都是眞要昇在告訴若薇亞公主那些他和克喜、阿米去過的地方，以及發生的故事。很快地，他們就變成像一對情侶一樣。

　　有一天，克喜告訴大家：

　　「日子很近了，波理斯瑪再過四十八個小時就要被毀滅了。」

Princess Rovia had a golden glow around her body. Her blue hair, when blown by the wind, would flow like water. She was kind, swift, and eager. Everyone in Purisima loved her. Alas, she was a young woman with a trouble on her mind, though.

TruEthan fell in love with her at first sight.

"Welcome to Purisima! I am Princess Rovia."

"P-P-Pretty. I... I am TruEthan."

"I hope you like Purisima, my homeland."

"It's a spectacular place! No other Jumpers can compare!"

"Really? I've never been to other Jumpers." Princess Rovia looked away, with a slight sorrow in her eyes. "I have never left Purisima."

That was the beginning of their conversation. TruEthan came back the next day to find Princess Rovia, and the day after, and the day after that. They would walk and talk for hours, mainly TruEthan was telling her about places and stories that Chrishie, Armi and himself had been to in Formonda. Soon enough they became like a couple.

One day Chrishie told the gang, "The day is near, Purisima will be destroyed in 48 hours."

「為什麼呢？」艾迪亞問。

「每一個跳越區都有自己的壽命。它們只能被摧毀，不能被延長。這在一開始用大十魔法創造的時候就是這樣設計的。」

真要昇問說：「我們可以帶若薇亞公主一起走嗎？」

「不行，她的命運就是要死在波理斯瑪的。」克喜回答。

那天晚上，真要昇去找若薇亞公主，他告訴她，當他們離開時，他會偷偷地帶著她一起走。若薇亞公主先是沒有說話，然後她告訴真要昇，卡爾王子正出外去打獵，不在波理斯瑪。

「但是我會很樂意和你一起走。」她說，隨著很小聲的一句「謝謝」，臉上閃過一抹興奮的紅暈。

第二天，他們準備要離開。克喜跟大家說：

「要去樂凡第，一定要經過一個叫做『阿努比斯之臉』的險惡地方，那是一片廣大的沙漠。阿努比斯（埃及神話中的狐狼神）只在白天的時候起來，所以如果我們是在晚上經過，就可以安全過境。」

「我們為什麼不用你那個機器帶我們到樂凡第呢？」艾迪亞問。

"But why?" asked Adiale.

"Each Jumper has its own life cycle. They can only be destroyed but not extended. It's been designed this way when they were created with Dash."

TruEthan asked, "Can we take Princess Rovia with us?"

"No, it is her destiny to die," Chrishie answered.

That night, TruEthan went to find Princess Rovia. He told her that when they leave, he would secretly bring her along. She was silent for a while, then told TruEthan that her brother, Prince Kale, was currently out of Purisima for hunting.

"Yes, I would love to go with you," she responded, followed by a whispering of "thank you". A blush of excitement spread on her face.

The next morning they were prepared to leave. Chrishie said to everyone,

"To make it to La Frontier, we'll travel through the Face of Anubis. It is a vast desert. Anubis only rises at day. So if we cross it at night, we'll make it."

"Why can't we use your machine to get to La Frontier?" asked Adiale.

「我的蟲洞機器對於要前往的地方，必須要收集足夠的資料才能設定為目的地。我自己還沒有到過樂凡第，所以我沒有參數來設定。」

「真要昇呢？」克喜環視左右，問道。

「大概又在跟若薇亞約會吧！」阿米說。

「我來了！在這裡！」真要昇跑上小山丘。

真要昇昨晚一整晚都沒睡。他很努力挖了一個地下隧道，並且告訴若薇亞公主怎麼用它來逃離波理斯瑪。

這一幫人馬上動身，要前往樂凡第。在他們身後，一把火正在熊熊燃起，把這一片美麗的國度燒滅。

他們走了好幾個小時，直到他們看到一個牌子，上面寫著：「阿努比斯之臉」。

「就是這裡了！」克喜宣布說，「我們已經走了一半了。」

突然，小樹叢後面有一個悉悉簌簌的聲音，若薇亞公主從小樹叢後面現身出來。

PRINCESS
Rovia

"My machine needs to gather enough data in order to set up the wormhole for the destination. I haven't been to La Frontier myself, so I don't have the parameters."

"Where's TruEthan?" Chrishie looked around and asked.

"Probably dating with Rovia again," responded Armi.

"I'm here!" TruEthan said, running up the hill.

TruEthan did not sleep for the whole night. He worked hard on an underground tunnel and instructed Princess Rovia to escape using it.

This group of adventurers left, on their way to La Frontier. Behind them, a fire started and burned the kingdom of beauty.

They walked for hours and hours until they finally reached a sign that said "The Face of Anubis."

"Here is the desert," Chrishie announced. "We're half way to La Frontier."

Suddenly, there was a rustle in the bushes. Princess Rovia emerged from behind them.

第三章　**阿努比斯之臉**

「搞什麼？！」克喜大叫，「我不是說了，她的命運是要死在波理斯瑪的嗎？」

「對不起，克喜。」真要昇道歉，「但我就是沒辦法把她留在那裡見死不救。」

「啊！你破壞了佛夢達的演算法則了！！」

「呃……我看我們還是趕快閃人吧！」阿米悄聲地對艾迪亞說。

「真要昇！你把我的計畫都搞砸了！」克喜大叫。

他才剛說完，一個巨大的黑影陡地罩上他們這幫人。

「糟了！現在還是白天，也就是說……」

「沒錯，就是我，阿努比斯，埃及的大神！你們要不就打敗我，從這裡經過，要不就死在這裡。」

阿努比斯說完，開始向他們發射無數的弓箭及火球。克喜瞇眼時，看到一件奇怪的事——有一個小男孩在阿努比斯的肩膀上，一邊吃著蘋果一邊跳舞！

Chapter III   The Face of Anubis

"What?!" screamed Chrishie. "Didn't I tell you her destiny was to die?!"

"Sorry, Chrishie," TruEthan apologized. "But I just couldn't leave her behind."

"Ugh! You just broke the algorithm of Formonda!"

"Eh…, I think we'd better slip away," Armi whispered to Adiale.

"My plan is officially ruined by you, TruEthan!"

Just as Chrishie finished saying that, a shadow cast over the group of travelers.

"Oh no!" said Chrishie. "It's still day, which means that is…"

"Me, Anubis! The Great Egyptian God! Defeat me and you will pass this land, or die."

After Anubis finished saying that, he started throwing arrows and fireballs at them. Chrishie squinted his eyes and saw something strange — a boy was dancing on Anubis's shoulder while eating an apple!

「啊啊啊！」艾迪亞一邊尖叫，一邊試著找地方躲藏。

「用爾卓式！」老人戴天尼大喊。

艾迪亞想起來之前老人戴天尼教她的，然後她就開始做手勢，使用這個法力。這一次老人戴天尼跟著她一起做，但是用另一種不同的手勢。電漿從艾迪亞手中噴射出來。

「可惡！」阿努比斯喊著說，然後在電漿擊中他之前即時消失了。

眾人歡喜若狂，大聲叫著：

「艾—迪—亞！艾—迪—亞！艾—迪—亞！」每個人都雀躍地把艾迪亞當英雄一般對待。

「當我在用爾卓式的時候，你為什麼用另一個不同的手勢呢？」艾迪亞問老人戴天尼。

「因為我們只是要對付阿努比斯，但不要摧毀其他的東西。所以我幫你的法力加上限制，把它控制住。」

「對了，那個吃蘋果的男孩在哪裡？」克喜問。

「這裡！這裡！」那個男孩叫著，「蘋果！蘋果！跳個曼波！」

「我知道你們要幹嘛！因為我一直從阿努比斯的水晶魔球上看你們一切發生的事。」

"Aaaaah!" Adiale screamed, trying to find somewhere to hide.

"Use Adro!" shouted Derteinium.

Adiale was reminded of what she was taught. Then she started using that move. This time Derteinium joined with a different hand movement. The plasma was ejected from Adiale's hands.

"Damn!" Anubis shouted and disappeared right before the power reached him.

The whole group was so happy and shouted,

"Adiale! Adiale! Adiale!" Everyone was cheering and treating Adiale as a hero.

"Why did you use a different move when I was using Adro?" Adiale was curious.

"Because we just wanted to kill Anubis but not everything else. So I added more control to that power."

"Anyway, do you know where the boy eating an apple is?" Chrishie asked.

"Here! Here!" the boy shouted. "Apple! Apple! Dance and ripple!"

"I know all about your quest, because I watch you on Anubis's magic ball," said the little boy.

「你叫什麼名字？你的家人呢？」克喜問道。

「我的名字叫布理布理。我在五歲的時候被阿努比斯從樂凡第綁架來這裡，讓我作他的送信者。我的家人住在可愛怡島上，你可以幫忙我找到我的家人嗎？」

「當然可以啊，小傢伙！」真要昇回答說，「我們現在正要去樂凡第呢！為了要幫你找到你的家人，我們必須知道你們家的姓氏。布理布理，你姓什麼？」

「可愛怡。我的全名是布理布理·可愛怡。這是全世界最富有的一個家族！」

「什麼？！你是可愛怡家族的人？天啊！真是太棒了！」真要昇驚奇地說。

"What's your name, little boy? Where's your family?" asked Chrishie.

"My name is Bri-Bri. I was abducted by Anubis from La Frontier when I was five. He made me his messenger. My family lives on Island of Kawaii. Can you help me find my family?"

"Of course we can, little dude!" TruEthan responded. "We're going to La Frontier right now! In order to find your family, we need to know your family name. What's your last name, Bri-Bri?"

"Kawaii. I am Bri-Bri Kawaii. Yes, the richest family in this world."

"What? You're in the Kawaii family? OMG! That's awesome!" TruEthan was impressed.

第四章　布理布理的故事

　　這是一個很安靜的夜晚，布理布理躺在床上，他的媽媽正幫他把棉被蓋好。

　　「乖寶寶，好好睡！」她在布理布理的額頭上親了一下。「不管你在哪裡，永遠都是媽媽的小布理布理，我的愛永遠都不會變。」

　　媽媽說的這些話讓布理布理覺得很幸福，她總是很慈愛。但不知怎地，今天這些話布理布理聽起來覺得有點神祕感，有一種黑暗及不安的感覺把他包圍起來。

　　「我愛你！明早見！」媽媽輕聲說著，離開房間，把門關上。

　　就在布理布理快要睡著的時候，一個黑影從窗外閃過。

　　「那是什麼東西？」布理布理發抖起來。

　　他的房門有響聲，開了一個小縫。一個影子迅速地飛進來。

　　「是我，阿努比斯。」

Chapter IV **The Story of Bri-Bri**

It was a quiet night. Bri-Bri's mom had just tucked him into bed.

"Be good, sleep tight!" she kissed his forehead. "Wherever you are, you will always be my little Bri-Bri and my love will never change."

Bri-Bri's mom said these words soothingly to Bri-Bri. She cared, of course, but it also sounded mysterious to Bri-Bri. A feeling of darkness and restlessness was wrapping around him.

"I love you. See you in the morning," she said gently and closed the door behind her.

Just as Bri-Bri was about to fall asleep, a shadow moved across the window.

"What was that?" Bri-Bri shuddered.

There was a rumble at the door, then the door creaked open. A shadow flew in and said,

"It is me, Anubis."

「啊——」布理布理還沒來得及叫出聲，阿努比斯已經把一個袋子套在他頭上。

「我要把你帶走。」阿努比斯獰笑說。

然後，阿努比斯就往外飛走，把布理布理帶回到他的金字塔去了。

天還沒亮，布理布理的媽媽從惡夢中驚醒過來。她趕緊跑去布理布理的房間，看到了一張紙條，是用血寫的字：

「阿努比斯 :1 」

她嚇壞了，撲倒在布理布理的床上，大聲哭喊著：

「不要！我親愛的布理布理！」

可愛怡先生衝進來，看到了那張紙條。

「啊！阿努比斯！」

之後，他們在布理布理的房間裡做了一個紀念小壇，上面擺著他的照片，旁邊圍繞著鬱金香。然後，他們走出去，向所有住在樂凡第跳越區的可愛怡家族的人們說：

「我們的兒子被阿努比斯擄走了！我們在這裡很不安全。我們全部的人都必須遷徙到『阿努比斯之臉』 北邊，那裡是我們可愛怡家族的應許之地，我們祖先的亡靈在那裡可以保護我們。我們必須生存下去，並且努力找到我的兒子！」

"Aaah — " before Bri-Bri finished screaming, Anubis tossed a bag over his head.

"I'm going to take you away," Anubis grinned.

Anubis flew outside with Bri-Bi, heading back to his pyramid.

Before dawn, Bri-Bri's mom woke up from a nightmare. She rushed to Bri-Bri's bedroom where she found a note, written in blood,

"AnUbis :l"

She freaked out and threw herself onto Bri-Bri's bed.

"Nooooooo! My dear Bri-Bri!" she cried out.

Mr. Kawaii ran in. "Oh no!" He shouted, "Anubis!"

Later, they built a shrine in Bri-Bri's room with his picture on a table, surrounded by tulips. Then, they went outside and spoke to all the Kawaii people living in the Jumper of La Frontier.

"Our son is abducted by Anubis! We are no longer safe in La Frontier. We must migrate to the north side of the Face of Anubis. That's the promise land for Kawaii family and our ancestors' spirits can protect us there. We must survive and strive to find my son!"

阿努比斯聽到這消息，從他的寶座上跳起來。

「哼，是嗎？」他不屑地笑著。

阿努比斯一直嫉妒可愛怡家族的富有及所受到的敬重，所以他把布理布理擄來，為他工作。他用許多的蘋果當作給他的工資，因為蘋果是布理布理最喜歡的食物。

布理布理成為阿努比斯的「威赫送信者」，這個工作是幫阿努比斯把可怕的惡夢放進人們的睡夢中。在這些年間，布理布理已經學會如何駭進人們的夢裡，藉由這樣的方式來傳遞信息。

當克喜這幫人遇到阿努比斯的時候，布理布理已經八歲了。在要攻擊他們之前，阿努比斯正要吃蘋果。布理布理從他的頭上跳下來偷走了他的蘋果，跑到外面去，邊吃邊跳舞。阿努比斯就把布理布理抓起來，放在肩膀上，接著去攻擊克喜那幫人。

Anubis jumped up on his throne when he heard this.

"Oh really…?" he smirked.

Anubis was always jealous of the wealth and respect that the Kawaii family had, so he decided to abduct Bri-Bri and make him work for him. He paid the little boy with lots of apples because that's Bri-Bri's favorite food.

Bri-Bri worked as a "Threat Messenger" whose job was to deliver nightmares in people's dreams. In those years Bri-Bri had learned how to send messages by hacking into people's dreams.

At the time when Chrishie and the group of travelers ran into Anubis, Bri-Bri was already eight years old. Anubis was going to eat an apple just before the attack. Bri-Bri jumped down from his head and stole the apple. He ran outside and started dancing. Anubis grabbed Bri-Bri, put him on his shoulder, and went to attack the travelers.

第五章 雷電市集

經過一陣簡短的介紹之後，這群人繼續他們的行程。幾天之後，他們到達樂凡第。

「哇！」每個人都驚訝地倒吸了一口氣。這裡的確是個富有的地方，到處都是擁有高爾夫球場和河上遊艇的豪宅。

「我家！」這時候布理布理突然大喊，然後往第一個漂浮的島嶼跑去，那上面有一棵大樹。

當大家隨後趕上布理布理的時候，他正坐在一棵樹旁哭泣，樹旁有一個牌子，上面寫著：「可愛怡之島」。他抬頭看那個牌子，眼裡充滿了盼望，但很快地又把頭低下去，瞪著地面。他的家已經人去樓空，他只看到在他自己的房間裡面，那個他爸媽為他做的紀念小壇。他所認識的族人也都不知去向了。

克喜跟阿米注意到了布理布理的沮喪，他們討論了一下，想要找個有趣的事情來做，好分散他的注意力。

「布理布理，在樂凡第哪裡有好玩的地方？」克喜問。

Chapter V Thunder Market

After the short introduction, the group of travelers went on. After a few days, they arrived at La Frontier.

"Whoa!" gasped everyone. This is definitely a place of wealth. There were mansions everywhere, with big golf courses and river boats.

"My Home!" Bri-Bri burst out. Then he started running toward the first floating island, the one with a big tree.

When the group finally caught up with Bri-Bri, he was sitting next to the tree, crying. There was a sign said "Island of Kawaii". He glanced up at the sign hopefully, but then stared back down at the ground. His home was empty now. He only found the altar that his parents set up in his bedroom. The Kawaii people that he knew were all gone.

Chrishie and Armi noticed Bri-Bri's depression. They discussed how to distract him with something fun.

"Bri-Bri, is there anything fun here in La Frontier?" asked Chrishie.

布理布理抬起頭，說：「雷電市集！以前小時候我爸媽常帶我去那裡逛。」

雷電市集是一個超巨大的市集，總長將近十英哩，位於雲端上面。在那裡有各式各樣的玩意兒，像是從最新的智慧型手機，到古老壁穴裡的畫。克喜想，如果讓每個人都買一個小禮物，他們的心情會好一點。於是他們就出發，搭乘城裡的高速雲端電梯。

他們到了之後，稍稍瀏覽一下這個雷電市集裡面各式各樣新奇有趣的生意，就知道這裡真是一個逛街購物的好地方。這裡不時有霹靂閃電照亮整個天空，就像在派對上放煙火一樣。

他們流連了一陣子之後，決定要在一個叫做「史卡達麵館」的餐廳吃午飯。他們在那裡互相展示觀看彼此剛剛買到的東西：克喜買的是一個可以改變聲音的機器，真要昇買了一本關於佛夢達所有跳越區歷史的書，若薇亞公主買了一雙球鞋，阿米買的是一個可穿透 20 英哩的超級手電筒，老人戴天尼買了一顆小樹苗，艾迪亞買的是一個霹靂閃電。

「怎樣？！」艾迪亞說，「買個霹靂閃電有什麼好奇怪的嗎？」

所有的人都睜大眼睛，瞪著它看。

「你們到底是有什麼問題？」艾迪亞說，很不高興地踱步走開。

Bri-Bri lifted his head and said, "Thunder Market! I used to go there with my parents when I was small."

So Bri-Bri led the way and brought the crew to the Thunder Market.

Thunder Market was a gigantic market place about 10 miles long. It was located on a cloud. They sold everything there, from the latest smartphones to ancient cave drawings. Chrishie thought that if they each get a little gift, their spirits would rise a bit. So they set off, using a high-speed Cloud-End escalator built in the city.

When they got there and caught a glimpse of all kinds of fun businesses in the market, they knew this would be a nice place for shopping. Thunderbolts lit up the sky like fireworks at a big party.

They roamed around a bit before deciding to have lunch at *Spagata Italiano*, where they had spaghetti. They shared what they had each bought. Chrishie bought a new machine that can change a person's voice. TruEthan bought a book that tells the history of every Jumper in Formonda. Princess Rovia bought a pair of sneakers. Armi bought a super flashlight that can penetrate as far as 20 miles. Derteinium bought a sapling. Adiale bought a thunderbolt.

"What?" Adiale said, "What's wrong about buying a thunderbolt?"

　　布理布理用他為阿努比斯工作時偷偷藏起來的私房錢買了一個 3D 列印機。

　　「你要怎麼帶著這個 3D 列印機？」真要昇問他。

　　「很簡單。」布理布理一邊說一邊很快地從克喜的背包裡拿出機器。

　　「用蟲洞。」

　　「不行！」克喜大叫。

　　就在克喜可以反應過來之前，布理布理已經把他買的 3D 列印機丟進正在打開的蟲洞裡。克喜非常地不高興，因為他很擔心這樣沒有設定目的地就把這個 3D 列印機亂丟進去，會讓它在時空連續帶之中搞丟。更糟的是，它有可能會把蟲洞弄破，造成裂縫，這表示蟲洞有可能會任意地把一些人亂吸進來。

The others stared, wide eyes.

"What's the problem with you people?" Adiale asked, storming away.

Bri-Bri bought himself a 3-D printer, with the money that he had kept a secret from Anubis when he was working for him.

"How are you going to bring that with you?" TruEthan asked.

"Easy," Bri-Bri said. He quickly grabbed the wormhole machine from Chrishie's backpack.

"Use the wormhole."

"No!" Chrishie shouted.

Just before Chrishie could react, Bri-Bri had thrown the 3-D printer into the wormhole that was just opening. Chrishie was very upset because he was afraid without coordinating the destination, the 3-D printer would get lost in the space-time continuum, and even worse, might make a crack in the wormhole. *That means the wormhole will suck random people in!*

第六章　覆蓋大地的黑暗

　　這時候，若薇亞公主想起了她的哥哥，卡爾王子。想到他現今不知在哪裡，她有點感傷。突然她的頭痛起來，若薇亞公主不自覺哀哼了一聲。

　　「妳還好嗎？」真要昇馬上察覺不對勁。

　　「嗯，還好。」若薇亞公主回答。

　　艾迪亞此時跑回來。

　　「有一股黑暗正在攻擊這裡！」她的聲音刺穿了夜空。「黑暗已經覆蓋這整個地方了！」

　　「天啊……」真要昇喊著。

　　「這下事情大條了！」阿米接著真要昇沒說完的話。

　　「快跑！」布理布理大叫。

　　混亂中，到處響起玻璃打碎在地上的聲音，人們倉皇逃命。克喜趕忙帶著這群人跳進蟲洞，他們在那裡稍微喘一口氣，從剛才的緊張狀況裡漸漸恢復正常。

　　「我們要去哪裡？」艾迪亞喘著氣問。

Chapter VI A Darkness That Covers the Land

At that moment Princess Rovia started to think about her brother, Prince Kale. She felt a little sad not knowing where he was. All of a sudden, her brain started to hurt. She gave a little shriek of pain.

"Are you okay, Rovia?" TruEthan noticed immediately.

"Uh, fine," Princess Rovia replied.

Adiale came running back to the group.

"A darkness is attacking!" Her voice pierced the still night air. "The darkness has covered the land all over!"

"Oh, no…," TruEthan said.

"It's a biggie," Armi finished TruEthan's sentence.

"Run!" Bri-Bri shouted.

After a crash of glass that broke to a million pieces on the ground, the group fled for their lives. Chrishie hurried the group into the wormhole. There, they started to relax and recover from the panic they had.

"Where are we going now?" Adiale said, still panting.

「去可愛怡聖壇！」布理布理變得很興奮。「我的整個家族都搬到那裡去了。我剛剛在那棵大樹上看到這段記錄。」

克喜查看佛夢達的地圖，還好可愛怡聖壇就在樂凡第旁邊。他點點頭，把蟲洞機器的目的地設定到兩個跳越區交接的邊境。

這時克喜突然想起一件事——他並沒有看見布理步理之前丟進蟲洞裡的那台 3D 列印機。他開始感到焦慮不安，不知道它跑到哪裡去了，會不會造成什麼後果。接著，很響的「噹」的一聲打斷了他的思緒，隨之而來的是一陣振動。有一個人突然憑空出現在他們面前，臉上顯出莫名其妙的表情。

「蝦肉？！」真要昇驚訝地說。

蝦肉很高興看到真要昇，他擁抱了真要昇、克喜和阿米。然後他看著其他人，一臉困惑。

「這些人是誰？他們是你的朋友嗎？」他問克喜。

「是的，」克喜回答，「你以後會有機會慢慢認識他們。你何不自我介紹一下?」

「好吧！」蝦肉說。

"Let's go to Kawaii Altar!" Bri-Bri exclaimed, becoming excited. "My entire family has moved there. I just saw that recorded on the Big Tree."

Chrishie looked at the map of Formonda. Luckily, Kawaii Altar was right next to La Frontier. He nodded his head and set up the destination to the border.

Then something came up to Chrishie's mind — he noticed that the 3-D printer that Bri-Bri threw in earlier wasn't here in the wormhole! He started to feel anxious. His was not sure where it had gone and what it would bring. His thought was interrupted by a loud zinging noise, followed by a zap. Then, a person stood right there wondering where he was.

"Sharo?!" TruEthan shouted.

Sharo was happy to see TruEthan. He hugged him, Chrishie, and Armi. Then he looked at the others and seemed confused.

"Who are these people?" he asked Chrishie. "Are they your friends?"

"Yes," Chrishie responded. "You will get to know them. Why don't you introduce yourself first?"

「我的名字是蝦肉，我還搞不清楚我怎麼會跑到你們
這裡來的。我本來住在日本，然後到德國去找我表哥，他
跟著他爸爸因爲太平洋戰爭的關係而搬到那裡去。有一天
我在公園裡碰到一個奇怪的人，他的名字叫安卓・藍普
提。他說了一些奇怪的字，聽起來像是：Who-You-You-
Who。我就是這樣到了佛夢達這個世界，然後認識了克
喜，眞要昇，和阿米。我們一起在佛夢達旅行了一陣子，
然後我決定要留在芬溪那個跳越區，所以我們就分手了。
在被吸進這個蟲洞之前，我正在芬溪搭火車。」

　　他才剛說完這番話，蟲洞打開了。他們看到的是一個
繁忙且便捷的大城市。

"Okay. My name is Sharo. I have no clue how I end up here. Anyway, I'm originally from Japan. I went to Germany to visit my cousin, whose dad moved there because of the Pacific War. Then I met a strange man in the park. His name was Andrew Lamputi. He said these mysterious words that sounded like: 'Who-You-You-Who'. That's how I entered this world of Formonda and met Chrishie, TruEthan, and Armi. We travelled together in Formonda for a while. Then I decided to stay in Fancì, so we parted. I was just riding on a train when I was sucked into this wormhole."

Just as he finished that sentence, the wormhole opened. They found themselves staring at a big and busy city full of activities and convenience.

第七章 # 因為夢

可愛怡聖壇有許多各式各樣的商店、住宅區、及公寓。他們看起來都非常現代，同時也充滿可愛、舒適的氣氛。道路繁忙，擁擠著汽車及行人。街道蜿蜒曲折，像個迷宮一樣。

他們終於來到可愛怡族人們居住的首都，打聽關於布理布理家人的訊息。然後才得知布理布理的爸爸媽媽為了尋找他，已經準備了三年，昨天才剛剛離開出發。布理布理聽了驚駭不已。

那天晚上睡覺時，布理布理心裡想，希望他在阿努比斯的那段時間都只是一場夢，而當這場夢結束時，他會在他自己原來溫馨的家裡醒過來，就在可愛怡島上，那個他溫暖舒服的房間裡。

但是並沒有。那天晚上他在夢裡得到的是一個異象。

「到大地的邊緣去。」那個異象說，「你的家人做了一個承諾，去觸摸那個承諾，你就會找到那條路。」

第二天早上醒來後，布理布理把這個夢告訴克喜。克喜找蝦肉一起來解夢，得到了以下的結論：

Chapter VII For the Dream

In Kawaii Altar, there were many different types of shops, townhouses, and apartments. They all looked very modern and filled up with cuteness and cuddliness. Roads were busy and crowded with cars and pedestrians. The streets twisted and turned and it seemed like a labyrinth.

When they finally found their way and reached the capital where the Kawaii people lived, they found out that Bri-Bri's mom and dad had been planning for three years to search for him and had just left a day ago! Bri-Bri was shocked.

That night, lying on his bed, Bri-Bri wished his time at Anubis was only a dream and he would wake up in his cozy bedroom on the cozy island of Kawaii, where he came from.

But he didn't. Instead, he had a vision in his dream.

"Go to the far end of this land," the vision said. "Your family made a promise. Touch the promise and there, will you find the way."

Bri-Bri told Chrishie about the dream when he woke up. Chrishie asked Sharo to help in decoding the dream. This was what he figured:

「到可愛怡聖壇和林特魁司這兩個跳越區交界的地方。那裡有一個聖門，上面放有布理布理的照片。觸摸那個門，它會打開。裡面有一個戒指，是布理布理的媽媽留下來的戒指，它會帶你們尋找到她。」

這群人於是前往林特魁司，路上遭遇到各式各樣的怪事，從飛龍到吸塵器的廣告都有。他們旅行了大約一百英哩左右，來到了邊界。那裡看起來像是個被遺棄的地方，到處都是形狀怪異、看起來很邪惡的樹，和烏鴉刺耳的尖叫聲。

這裡到處都是魔法，甚至比一個百分之百的神話故事還有更多的魔法！在紅外線照射下即可打開許多漩渦入口，還有許多看不見的鬼魂在到處遊盪。

終於，他們來到一塊大石頭前面，上面有些彫刻的圖案。布理布理盯著它看，當克喜正要說：「退後！」的時候，一個漩渦入口突然出現。在那個漩渦入口裡面有一扇門，門上有布理布理的照片。布理布理輕輕地摸著照片，想起媽媽幫他拍這張照片的那一天，眼淚從他的兩頰掉了下來。

門打開了，裡面有一個戒指，旁邊還有一個紙卷。布理布理把戒指拿起來，套進自己的手指。克喜拿起那個紙卷，小心翼翼地把它展開，以免它遭到破壞。紙卷裡面有一個人的照片，不是別人，而是艾迪亞！

Go to the border of Kawaii Altar and Lintercrest. There is a sacred door with Bri-Bri's picture on it. Touch the door and it will open. There is a ring that belongs to Bri-Bri's mom and can lead the way to her.

When the group left for Lintercrest, they encountered all sorts of things, from dragons to advertisements for vacuum cleaners. They traveled about a hundred miles to get themselves to the border. When they got there, they saw it was abandoned. The only things there were wretched trees and shrieking crows.

The magic was flowing everywhere, more than even a one hundred percent fairytale story. Portals opened up in infrared light. Many invisible ghosts were roaming the place.

Finally, they reached a stone engraved with some carvings. Bri-Bri stared at it. Chrishie was about to say, "Move back!" when a portal appeared. In the portal was a door, engraved with a picture of Bri-Bri. Bri-Bri touched it gently, remembering the day when his mother took this picture, tears rolled down his cheeks.

The door opened, and there was a ring, next to a scroll. Bri-Bri took the ring and slid it onto his finger. Chrishie took the scroll and opened it carefully, hoping to preserve it. There was a single picture of no one else, but Adiale!

艾迪亞非常吃驚,她不明白為什麼這裡面會有她的照片。

這表示我和布理布理的家族肯定有些什麼關連。她這樣想。

蝦肉也很吃驚,也許此刻我們可以叫他「嚇蝦」。但那是假的,蝦肉只是看起來(或裝得)很震驚。蝦肉是那種直覺很強、很能把線索連貫起來的人。他曾經去過可愛怡聖壇的「顯赫博物館」,他知道在預言中會有一個可愛怡家族的拯救者。他當時看到一塊石板,上面寫到將會有另外兩個人,來自另一個世界相反的兩個地方,來幫助這個拯救者。

現在這一切在他眼裡已經很明顯,關於艾迪亞的來到佛夢達,還有為什麼紙卷上會有她的照片。

Adiale was shocked. She wondered why there was a picture of her on that scroll.

It must mean I am connected with Bri-Bri's family somehow! She thought.

Sharo was shocked, too. Maybe for now we can call him double S, or SS (for Shocked Sharo). But he was just showing (or pretending) that he was shocked. Sharo was the kind of person who liked to see the big picture, and also very intuitive. He had visited the Grand Museum in Kawaii Altar before. He learned that there would be a "Savior of Kawaii" in the prophecy. He saw a stone slab that said there would be two more people from the opposite sides of another world to help this savior.

Now it seemed obvious to him, about Adiale's coming here to Formonda and why the scroll had her picture.

第八章 強柯勒萬

　　話說這群人，他們再次回到可愛怡聖壇的首都。他們決定在漫長辛苦的搜尋之後，要好好休息一下。

　　克喜準備上床就寢，輪到蝦肉要去洗澡（除了若薇亞公主之外，他們全都住在同一個房間）。正當他快要洗完時，一個「喀拉喀拉」的響聲搖晃了整棟建築物，外面走廊上一陣強風「颼颼」刮過，那巨大的響聲就像是高功率的立體音響調到最大音量時那麼刺耳。

　　燈光忽暗忽明地閃動著，門被風吹開了。門口站著一個人影，周圍環繞著黑暗，空氣中有一股很濃的酒精味。

　　「我，是強柯勒萬。」那個人說。

　　可怕的黑暗之臂往前伸出，伴隨著一個大大的鬼牌傑克的獰笑。

　　「我就是黑暗！」

　　蝦肉睜大了眼，手中的牙刷掉到地上，這下他是真的變成「嚇蝦」了！阿米快要哭出來，布理布理已經躲到毯子底下去了。

Chapter VIII   **Jrunk Lerwan**

The group returned to the capital of Kawaii Altar again. They decided after a big and long day of questing, it was time to rest.

Chrishie had begun to settle down for some sleep. It was Sharo's turn to shower (except for Princess Rovia, they all stayed in the same room). Just as he was finishing up, a rattling shook the building. The sound of wind was swishing through the hallways outside, as loud as a surround sound speaker turned on full blast.

The lights were flashing. The door flew open. There stood a figure, surrounded by darkness. There was a strong smell of alcohol in the air.

"I, am Jrunk Lerwan," he said.

Arms of darkness started to reach out, with a big Joker smile.

"I am the darkness."

Sharo stared wide eyed and dropped his tooth brush. For once he really became an SS. Armi was starting to cry. Bri-Bri hid himself under a blanket.

「蘋果，蘋果⋯⋯跳個曼波⋯⋯？」布理布理嚇得語無倫次。

連已經睡著的艾迪亞都被驚醒了。

「是誰這麼吵？！」她大喊。但是當她睜開眼睛時，她的臉色頓時轉成慘白。

突然之間，一片黑暗！沒有人昏倒，而是停電了。

若薇亞公主在隔壁房間聽到這一切。這時候黑暗力量變形成為許多碎片，從門縫裡爬進若薇亞公主的房間。當她看到時嚇得跳起來，這些黑暗碎片緊緊纏住她的腳，她失去平衡，跌在地上，死了。

沒有人知道在這一段停電時發生了什麼事。等到一切都安靜下來，強柯也離去了，大家來到若薇亞公主的房間找她，他們看到她躺在地上。

真要昇說不出一句話，呆呆地站在那裡，一片空白。然後淚水開始從他的眼裡湧出，他傷心地啜泣著，在若薇亞公主的身邊坐下來。

「你們都去睡覺吧！我想要坐在這裡陪她到早上。」他說。然而幾個小時之後他也睡著了。

"Apple, apple, dance and ripple...?" Bri-Bri whispered while being freaked out completely.

Even Adiale who was asleep had to wake up.

"Who Is Making That NOISE?!" she shouted, but when she opened her eyes, her face went pale.

Suddenly, everything went black. No one fainted. It was a blackout.

Princess Rovia was listening from the room next to Chrishie's. Pieces of darkness started to crawl into her room. She jumped back when she saw them. Those pieces of darkness trapped her feet tightly. She lost her balance and fell to the ground, dead.

No one knew what happened in the blackout. After things quieted down and Jrunk left, they went to check on Princess Rovia. They found her body on the floor.

TruEthan could not say a thing. He stood there, seemingly blank. Then, tears started to well up in his eyes. He sobbed sadly and sat down next to the body of Princess Rovia.

"You people go to sleep. I want to stay with her till morning," he said. But he fell asleep a couple of hours later.

第二天早上，若薇亞公主醒來，搞不清楚自己到底發生了什麼事（我知道你在想什麼——沒錯，她已經死了，但她的靈魂仍在）。她看到真要昇在那裡睡著，然後她晃到克喜的房間 。蝦肉抬起眼，剛好看到她，頓時他的眼中閃耀著希望的光芒。若薇亞公主覺得奇怪，為什麼蝦肉那樣看著她，她低頭看看自己，才意識到自己變成一團朦朧的霧，而且已經死了。

這時候，蝦肉得到一個啟示：從現在開始，他們尋找布理布理家人的這個任務，若薇亞公主將會成為一個引導者。他告訴大家這個啟示。真要昇很高興，至少他現在仍然可以看到若薇亞公主，她仍然可以跟著他們一起去旅行。

因為強柯的關係，他們知道自己現在身處危險。於是他們起身，準備出發去尋找布理布理的父母。若薇亞公主的鬼魂就跟著他們一起。

In the morning, Princess Rovia woke up, not knowing what she was (I know what you're thinking— yes, she was dead, but her spirit was alive). She saw TruEthan sleeping there, then wandered to Chrishie's room. Sharo looked up at Princess Rovia, hope glimmering in his eyes. She looked down at herself, wondering why Sharo was looking at her. Suddenly she realized she was only a blur and that she was dead.

There, Sharo got the insight that Princess Rovia from now on would become a guide on this quest to find Bri-Bri's family. He shared this with the group. TruEthan was so comforted and happy that he at least could still see some bit of Princess Rovia and she could still travel with them, together.

Now they knew they were in danger because of Jrunk. The group started to rise and get ready for the journey in search of Bri-Bri's parents. The ghost of Princess Rovia followed them.

第九章 # 黑洞

　　這群人匆忙地離開，他們盡量躲躲藏藏，因為到處都有強柯的眼線。他們夜以繼日，走了好多天，鞋子都差不多磨破了。對若薇亞公主公主來說倒是很輕鬆容易， 一點也不費力，因為她是個鬼魂。

　　他們又累又餓。終於有一天，他們來到一個小城，城裡有個餐廳，還有好吃的蛋糕。他們吃了好多好多食物，當他們吃完，準備要離開時，他們看到一個人影擋在前面，背對著他們。

　　「嘖，嘖，嘖，」這個人說，「被嚇壞的小貓啊～」

　　他轉過身來，一個陰險的笑容在他的臉上散開來。他穿著一個暗色的風衣，頭上戴著一頂很大的黑色牛仔帽，他的眼睛被大帽子的陰影遮住。然後，那陰影漸漸移開，把他的臉給露出來。

　　「強柯勒萬！」大家高聲喊叫。

　　當他露出臉來的同時，他的風衣迅速地向外張開飛揚起來。傾刻間，這群人通通消失不見了。

　　強柯把他們放到一個黑洞裡面！

Chapter IX **Black Hole**

The group set off in a hurry. They tried their best to stay well-hidden because there might be spies for Jrunk anywhere. They walked for days and days, until their shoes were almost worn out. It was easy for Princess Rovia because she did not expend any energy as a ghost.

They were hungry and tired. Finally, they reached a nice little city with a restaurant and some nice cake, too. They ate tons of food. When they finished and were ready to leave, they saw a figure in front of them blocking their way, with his back to them.

"Well, well, well," he said. "The scaredy-cats, Eh?"

He turned around, an unfriendly smile creeping on his face. He was wearing a dark coat with a big black cowboy hat, his eyes lurking in shadows. Then the shadows started to move and make out a face.

"Jrunk Lerwan!" People were screaming.

Swiftly his coat flew open as he revealed who he was. Suddenly the group vanished.

Jrunk put them in a black hole!

在黑洞裡面的感覺跟你想像的完全不一樣──它吸收了太多的光，所以裡面變成絕對的明亮與一片白色。他們在黑洞裡什麼也看不到，因爲太亮了！他們很慌亂，因爲每個人都瞎了。

他們必須逃跑，克喜知道使用蟲洞可以幫忙逃離這裡，但問題是他什麼也看不到。他花了好長一段時間，藉由手的觸覺才把他的機器接上。

很幸運地，他們來到一條河邊。在他們還沒來得及搞清楚這是哪裡之前，他們聽到了腳步聲。他們怕是強柯的追趕，所以馬上就跳進水裡，屏住呼吸。他們看到一張臉，從水面上往下看。當他們實在憋不過氣來了，只好浮出水面，大大吸了一口氣。原來那個人只是一個男孩。

「嗨！」那個戴眼鏡的男孩興奮地說，「你們是誰？」

「將安！」阿米高聲喊著說，「眞的是你嗎？」

「喔！我的天啊！」將安這時候認出來克喜、阿米，和眞要昇，在這一堆奇怪的人裡面。「你們在水裡面搞什麼飛機啊？！裝死嗎？」他笑得很大聲。

The experience in the black hole was not what you would imagine. It absorbed so much light that it turned to absolute whiteness inside. They couldn't see anything in the brightness and panicked as they became literally blind.

They needed to escape. Chrishie knew that the wormhole machine could help. The problem was he could not see a thing. It took him a long time to finally connect the machine by means of his sense of touch.

Luckily they appeared by a river. Before they could figure out where they were, they heard footsteps. They were too afraid that Jrunk was chasing them, so they quickly jumped into the water and held their breath. They saw a face looking down at them from above. When they could no longer hold it, they swam up and gasped for breath. It turned out it was a mere boy.

"Hi!" the boy wearing glasses said excitedly. "Who are you?"

"John!" Armi exclaimed. "Is it really you?"

"Oh My God!" John recognizing Armi, Chrishie, and TruEthan in this odd group. "What the hell are you guys doing in the water?! Playing dead?" He laughed loudly.

第十章　水

　　艾迪亞很不喜歡將安。他笨手笨腳的，常常撞到別人，而且很喜歡對每件事做分析，說些別人聽不懂的結論。他甚至讓這一群人因為打賭而被迫跳到水裡去游泳。

　　艾迪亞對著將安吼著說：「你為什麼要因為打一個賭而讓我們在凍死人的河裡游泳？」

　　「喔，那當然，為了要贏這個賭啊！」他很悠哉地說。

　　「那是誰想到要打賭的？！」艾迪亞對著將安的耳朵尖叫。

　　「喂！是你自己輸了！」將安喊回去。

　　「嗯……哈囉？」克喜試著轉移他們的注意力。

　　「我們現在並不需要一個白癡哈囉！」艾迪亞轉過去對著克喜吼叫。

　　就在這時，水裡突然產生了一個連漪。那個連漪越來越大，最後變成一個大漩渦。所有的人都又驚又怕。然後有兩個美麗的女孩從漩渦的中央緩緩升起。

Chapter X **Waters**

Adiale didn't like John. He was clumsy and would bump into others every now and then. He also liked to analyze everything and gave conclusions that are hard to understand. He even made this group of travelers swim in the river because of a stupid bet.

Adiale was shouting at John. "WHY did you make us SWIM in a FREEZING RIVER because of a BET!"

"Well, of course, to win the bet," John said calmly.

"Well, WHOSE idea was it to BET?!" Adiale screamed in John's ears.

"WELL YOU LOST IT!" John screamed back at Adiale.

"Um… hello?" asked Chrishie, trying to grab their attention.

"WE DON'T NEED STUPID HELLOS RIGHT NOW!" Adiale yelled in Chrishie's face.

Just at this exact moment, the water started to ripple. It grew bigger and bigger, and it soon became a swirl. The group stared in awe as two beautiful girls started to rise from the center of the swirl.

「嗨！我的名字叫潔兒。」第一個女孩穿著淺綠色及白色的長衫。

「嗨！我的名字叫迷蝶。」第二個女孩穿著淺藍色及白色的長衫。

「我們是姊妹。」她們異口同聲地說。

「帥呀！」將安低聲說。

艾迪亞生氣地瞪著將安看。

布理布理看起來嚇壞了。阿米因為布理布理嚇到而感到驚嚇。真要昇看到他們都被嚇到，因而嚇到。克喜則是因為真要昇被嚇到而嚇到。蝦肉則是覺得這麼多人同時被嚇到在科學上是不可能的，而驚惶失措。

然後艾迪亞大叫：

「笨蛋！你們通通給我醒過來！你們到底是為什麼被嚇到？」

「呃……剛剛發生什麼了？」阿米問。

「我們應該趕快離開這個要命的鬼地方。」迷蝶說。

迷蝶和潔兒知道這個叫做「愚里客」的地方有一種魔法，會使人抓狂並出現奇怪的行為。

「說真的，你們這一群人在這裡幹什麼呢？」迷蝶問。

"Hi! My name is Jade," said the first girl who was wearing a gown in colors of light green and white.

"Hi! My name is Misty," said the second girl who was wearing a gown in colors of light blue and white.

"We're sisters," they said simultaneously.

"Ooooh, pretty!" John cooed.

Adiale stared at John in annoyance.

Bri-Bri looked horrified. Armi was horrified that Bri-Bri was horrified. TruEthan was horrified seeing that they both were horrified. Chrishie was horrified because TruEthan was horrified. Sharo was horrified that everyone being horrified at once wasn't scientifically possible.

Then Adiale screamed, "WAKE UP YOU STUPID PEOPLE, HOW DID YOU GET HORRIFIED IN THE FIRST PLACE?!"

"Uh… what just happened?" Armi asked.

"We should leave this freaky place," Misty said.

Misty and Jade knew that this place, called Urik, had a magic that caused people to go crazy with weird behaviors.

"Anyway, what are you doing here?" Misty asked.

「我們要幫布理布理，這個小老弟，找到他的家人。同時我們也在逃避一個叫做強柯的邪惡壞蛋，他擁有控制黑暗的魔法。」克喜回答。

「喔！那我們可以加入你們，去幫忙找布理布理的家人嗎？」迷蝶和潔兒問。

「當然囉！」克喜說。

「等一等！若薇亞公主呢？」眞要昇突然問。「我是說，她的鬼魂，在哪裡？」

"We are trying to help Bri-Bri, this little dude, find his family. But we're also trying to run away from an evil man that controls the darkness. His name is Jrunk," Chrishie replied.

"Oh, then can we join you to find Bri-Bri's family?" Misty and Jade asked.

"Sure," said Chrishie.

"Hold on! Where is Princess Rovia?" TruEthan suddenly asked. "I mean, her spirit."

第十一章　一首詩

　　他們開始找若薇亞公主，但是徒勞無功。事實上，她是被強柯抓去了。若薇亞公主試著要和眞要昇聯絡，於是她寫了一首詩，放在一片雲上面，漂了好長一段路，終於送到眞要昇手中。

∞

這是眞正的我自己

因著你而被表達出來

若不然，我就不存在

我吃下了那個蘋果

又甜又酸

又愛又恨

但你的愛像是一隻鴿子

乘著它的翅膀，我永遠不死

Chapter XI A Poem

They started searching for Princess Rovia, but failed. As a matter of fact, Princess Rovia was taken by Jrunk. Princess Rovia tried to contact TruEthan. She wrote a poem on a cloud which drifted a long way to reach TruEthan.

∞

This is my true self

Expressed, with your help

If not, I don't exist

I ate the apple

So sweet and sour

So admired and hated

But your love was like a dove

On its wings, I would never die

我也是一個蘋果，通紅似血

而你知道我愛好冒險的心

你把光明帶給我的黑影

照亮了我攀附著的懸崖

所以我活下來了

然而此刻死亡正在徘徊

沒有逃路

血會濺出更多的血

和平非常遙遠

∞

　　真要昇看了很感動，想寫個回信給若薇亞公主。但是他還是決定不要寫，因為他知道佛夢達最大的戰役就快要來了，他知道「血會濺出更多的血」是什麼意思——強柯會找到布理布理的家人而且把他們殺掉。這將會是一場硬仗！

　　那天晚上，真要昇寫著他的日記，感覺好像是世界末日要來了一樣。他寫道：

I was an apple, as red as blood

And you know my adventurous mind

You brought the light onto my shadow

Shinning on the cliff that I hung on to

So I survived

But now death is lingering

There is no escape

Blood will spill more blood

And the peace is far

∞

TruEthan was so touched and tempted to write back to Princess Rovia. But he decided not to because he knew the greatest battle of Formonda was coming. He knew what it meant by "blood will spill blood" — *Jrunk will find out where Bri-Bri's family is and destroy them. This is going to be hard-fought!*

On that night, TruEthan wrote in his own journal, feeling like it was the end of the world. This is what he wrote:

∞

　　親愛的若薇亞，但願我也能寫一首詩，可是我不會寫詩，所以這就是我給妳的情書了。沒有什麼其他事是比愛還更重要的。我將會乘著靈魂的風，旅行去尋找妳。我真希望我們能過一個普通的生活，至少是一個普通的冒險生活，因為我一直都知道妳心裡藏著一個想去冒險的渴望。但我了解到生活充滿了悲傷，我是否該說些有趣的話呢？是的，應該要，這個如何⋯⋯我吃了一個不幸長得像嘔吐物一樣的冰淇淋聖代。這好笑嗎？我不知道。我希望有一天當我再讀這些話的時候，會想起此刻的痛苦和悲傷，還有我們曾經分享過的愛。

　　你的摯愛，真要昇

Dearest Rovia, I wish I could write a poem, but I do not have that skill. So this is my love letter for you.

Nothing matters when it comes to love. I will travel on the Wind of the Soul to reach you. I wish we could have lived a normal life, or at least a normal adventurous life because I always know about your hidden desire for adventures. But I just realized that life is filled with sorrows.

Should I say something funny? I decided yes, here it is... I had an ice cream sundae that unfortunately looked like barf. Is that even funny? I can't tell. I wish I will read this again and remember the pain and sorrow — and the love we shared together.

Yours, TruEthan

第十二章 乘著靈魂之風

　　眞要昇和克喜討論關於尋找若薇亞公主的事。問題
是：她到底在哪裡？在佛夢達的世界裡有上百個跳越區，
有太多的可能性，比如說，追夢麗，中央希尼提府，費洛
費洛斯，馬系爾，倫丹艾夫瑞，等等。

　　「喂！大家注意！我們必須在佛夢達全境開始搜尋若
薇亞公主。」克喜宣佈。

　　「那布理布理的家人怎麼辦？」迷蝶提出問題。

　　「對呀！我的家人怎麼辦？」布理布理同意。

　　蝦肉說：「布理布理，若薇亞公主是引導我們去找你
的家人的關鍵。」

　　「是啦！」將安說，「蝦肉講的這一點是沒錯，但是
若薇亞公主是個鬼魂，只有鬼牆才能鎖住她，使她無法自
由穿梭。在佛夢達有上百個跳越區，我們怎麼知道她被鎖
在哪一個？我們能找到她的機會微乎其微，大概只有
0.72356498009172%。」

Chapter XII On the Wind of the Soul

TruEthan discussed with Chrishie about the task of searching for Princess Rovia. The question was: Where is she? There were hundreds of Jumpers in the world of Formonda, thus so many possibilities, like Dreamryl, Central Cinitifut, Phrosforous, Masil, Rendisten El Fore, etc.

"Hey! People! We will have to quest through Formonda to find Princess Rovia!" said Chrishie.

"What about Bri-Bri's family?" Misty challenged.

"Yeah! What about my family!" Bri-Bri agreed.

Sharo replied, "Princess Rovia is our *guide* to find your family, Bri-Bri."

"Well," said John, "Sharo is correct in this point. But, Rovia is a ghost, only 'ghost barriers' can keep her locked from traveling anywhere. There are hundreds of Jumpers in Formonda. How do we know which one she is locked in? The chance for us to find her is very, very, very low, approximately 0.72356498009172%."

「住嘴！」艾迪亞說。她就是對將安覺得很感冒。

「等一等！」蝦肉突然叫說：「我知道一個地方是有鬼牆的——勁剋司！」

「嗯……但是我們不能使用蟲洞去到那裡。」克喜自言自語地說：「我這個機器所產生的蟲洞是沒辦法穿越鬼牆的。當我們進入蟲洞的時候，我們其實就是產生一種質變，變得跟鬼魂很像，所以我們會浮起來，穿越很遠的地方。」

「還有另一個辦法。」很久沒有說話的老人戴天尼此時突然開口了。「有一個法力叫作『靈魂之風』，它可以穿透任何阻擋的牆。但是它只能被真愛啓動。」

「所以，只有真要昇可以啓動這個法力囉！」阿米說。

所有的人都看著真要昇，把希望寄託在他身上。

接下來幾個小時，老人戴天尼一直在教真要昇怎麼啓動這個特別的法力。當真要昇終於學會了，他就開始召喚這股「靈魂之風」。一開始他是感覺到頭髮下面有微風輕輕吹過，同時感到他的靈魂在愛與喜悅中跳著一支和諧的舞。這風越來越強，最後變成一個龍捲風，把每一個人都掃進去。

他們就乘著這股風，一路來到勁剋司。

"Shut up!" said Adiale. Somehow she just didn't get along with John.

"Wait!" Sharo shouted suddenly, "I know a place where there are ghost barriers — Zinx!"

"Hmm…. But we can't get there using the wormhole," Chrishie was thinking out loud. "The wormhole machine that we've been using can't penetrate ghost barriers. When we go into a wormhole, we actually go through a quality change and become sort of like ghosts. That is why we can float and travel such far distances."

"There is another way," the long-not-mentioned Derteinium spoke. "There is a power called 'the Wind of the Soul'. It can penetrate any type of barriers. But it can only be triggered with true love."

"So, only TruEthan can trigger it," Armi said.

Everyone was looking at TruEthan with hope.

For the next few hours Derteinium showed TruEthan how to trigger this special power. When TruEthan finally mastered it, he summoned "the Wind of the Soul". It started with him feeling a gentle breeze blow his hair, and his soul dancing in harmony with love and joy. The wind grew stronger and turned into a tornado that sucked everyone in.

They rode all the way on it to Zinx.

　　這個地方是個叢林。有許多的樹，被遺棄的礦場，死城，監獄，礦坑，還有最詭異的是——有一個核電廠！

This place was a jungle. There were trees, abandoned mines, ghost towns, jails, mineshafts, and the most weird of all — a nuclear power plant!

第十三章　夜晚駭客

「我覺得我們應該爬到那個電廠的管子上面去。」將安提議。

「可以啊。」克喜說。

「雖然有百分之五十六的機會我們會到不了。」將安的數學很好。

「呃……」克喜聽了之後開始變主意。

但他們還是這樣做了，因為大家都想要爬上一個高的地方去眺望一下這整個跳越區。當他們終於爬上去之後，他們看見在煙囪旁邊有一個很小的平台，他們就站在平台上，眺望勘查勁剋司這個跳越區。他們瞥見幾個看起來很可疑的地方，也許會是強柯藏匿若薇亞公主之處。他們攏靠在一起，討論著怎樣才能到那裡去。

除了潔兒之外，沒有人看到一個長得像是酷斯拉一樣的超大怪物正在向他們這裡移動，大概就只有三十公尺這麼近了。

Chapter XIII Hacker of the Night

"I say we climb the power plant's tube thing!" John suggested.

"Fine with me," said Chrishie.

"Though there is a 56% chance we will fail," added John, who was really good at mathematics.

"Umm…," Chrishie started to change his mind.

But they did it anyway because everyone wanted to climb somewhere high so they could have a look at the entire Jumper. When they climbed up and finally made it, they found a small deck next to the chimney. They stood on the deck, looking out and examining this Jumper, Zinx. They spotted some suspicious-looking areas that Jrunk might have hid Princess Rovia. They huddled together discussing ideas of how to get there.

Except for Jade, no one saw a gigantic monster that looked like Godzilla moving towards them, about 30 meters away.

「打打，耶耶，羅嘎……」那個怪物發出模糊不清的聲音。

「啊～啊～快跑！」潔兒大叫。

他們轉過身來，看到這個醜惡的怪物，都被嚇壞了！阿米嚇得渾身動彈不得，蝦肉第一時間就往煙囪跑去。

「跳進管子裡！」克喜喊著。

他們全都即時跳進去了，就在怪物把那個平台拆成碎片之前。

他們掉落在一堆煤炭上面，身上和臉上有幾處被刮傷。在煤炭坑旁邊的牆上有一個大洞，那是一個室內通風系統的通風口。他們屈身進去，在那個通風管裡往前爬。最後他們從另一端的通風口掉出來，摔到地上。他們用盡所有的力氣站起來，因為害怕那個怪物還在追他們，每個人都慌亂地跑向不同的地方，在建築物裡的各處逃竄，迷失了好一陣子。幸好，最後在一個會議室的門口大家又碰到一起，除了將安之外。

將安發現自己來到一個像是研究室的地方，裡面到處都寫著數學公式——在白板上，紙頁上，還有家俱上。他在房間裡邊走邊看這些公式。

"DADA EEE ROAH GA…," that monster was mumbling.

"Aaaaah! Run!" Jade screamed.

They turned around and were terrified by the ugly creature. Armi froze of terror. Sharo immediately ran toward the chimney.

"Jump inside the tube!" Chrishie shouted.

They all jumped inside the chimney, just in time, before the monster ripped off the deck.

They fell onto coal and got scrapes and scars. There was a big hole on the wall next to the coal chamber that led to the air ventilation system. They crouched into the vent and crawled. They dropped out of the vent and fell to the ground. They used all their energy to stand up. Fearing that the giant monster was still after them, everyone panicked and started running into different parts of the building. People were lost in different places, for a while. Fortunately, they all met together again outside a conference room, everyone but John.

John found himself coming to a room that looked like a research place, where mathematical equations were written everywhere — on the white board, on the paper, on the furniture. He walked around the room looking at those equations.

他聽到怪物沉重的腳步聲從窗外經過，於是他趕緊躲進一個大紙箱裡面。他把夾克脫下來，捲成一個枕頭，又把自己的手腳縮進毛衣裡，縮成像一團球一樣。因為非常疲憊，他很快就睡著了。

他夢到一大堆的數學公式，還有一些卡通人物，很忙碌地在擦掉那些公式。他看到其中有一個卡通人物一直盯著他看，然後漸漸向他漂移過來。

那是布理布理！

「你找到我了！」將安高聲喊。

「其實不是……我現在是駭入你的夢裡面。我來告訴你，我們現在通通聚在一個會議室裡面。我們會一直待到明天太陽下山的時候，你趕快過來找我們！」

布理布理的影像漸漸淡去，將安醒來了。他趕緊把上衣穿好，把夾克拉鍊拉上，走向門邊。他看著掛在門口旁的建築物平面圖。

下一個右轉，然後一直走，左轉，然後再一個往右的迴轉……喔！幹嘛那麼麻煩？就把這地圖帶走不就得了？

He heard the monster's footsteps stomping outside the window, so he quickly hid in a cardboard box. He took off his jacket and rolled it into a pillow. He tucked himself into his sweater and curled like a ball. Very soon he fell asleep because he was too tired.

He dreamed of lots of mathematic equations and some cartoon characters who were busy erasing those equations. Then he saw a cartoon character who was staring at him first, then started to drift toward him.

It was Bri-Bri!

"You have found me!" John exclaimed.

"Not really…. I am hacking into your dream now to tell you that we are all in a conference room. We will be waiting here 'till sundown tomorrow. Come over here as soon as possible!"

Bri-Bri's image started fading away. Then John woke up. He quickly put his sweater on and zipped up his jacket, and walked to the door of the room. He scanned the map that hung next to the door.

Next right turn, and walk until a left turn, and then a sharp right turn…. Oh, who am I kidding…. I'll just take the map.

他動手把那塊地圖的板子整個拆下來，走出去，來到走廊裡。他沿著廊道左彎右拐，然後看到一個門，上面掛著一個牌子，寫著「會議室」。

He yanked the map off the wall and walked outside into the hallway. He followed the hallway as it twisted and turned. Then he saw a door with a big sign on it. It said "Conference Room".

第十四章 **可愛怡夫婦的旅程**

　　可愛怡太太一邊走一邊含著淚水，她一想到布理布理就傷心得不得了。他已經失蹤三年了！她還記得她和老公一起帶著樂凡第的同鄉們搬到可愛怡聖壇的那一天。他們在那裡定居下來，並且把它發展成一個很繁榮的跳越區，但是她還是很想念他們原來在樂凡第的家。

　　可愛怡太太爬上了馬車，他們現在已來到富可寧這個跳越區南部的邊境。

　　「歐瑞（可愛怡先生的名字），你想現在吃午餐嗎？」

　　「別吧……」可愛怡先生回答，「我們會在博列姆停留吃飯，我聽說那裡有一個很高級的餐廳。」

　　「好吧……」可愛怡太太聽起來有點失望。

　　「妳還好嗎？梅莉（可愛怡太太的名字）。」

　　「我還好，只是有點心事。」

　　「什麼事？」

Chapter XIV **Kawaii's Journey**

Mrs. Kawaii walked forward with tears in her eyes. She was too sorrowful thinking about Bri-Bri. He had been missing for three years! She remembered the day she and Mr. Kawaii left La Frontier for Kawaii Altar and settled there. They established the Jumper so it became very prosperous. But she missed their old home back in La Frontier.

Mrs. Kawaii climbed up into the horse-drawn carriage. They were almost at the south border of Frecenìn by now.

"Hey, Orei (Mr. Kawaii's name), do you want to have lunch now?"

"Nay," said Mr. Kawaii. "We will stop by Blem for lunch. I heard they had a fine restaurant called *Bubbi*."

"Okay…," Mrs. Kawaii sounded disappointed.

"Are you okay, Melli (Mrs. Kawaii's name)?"

"Yeah, I'm fine. I just got something on my mind."

"Well, what is it?"

「喔，沒什麼。歐瑞，你還記得布理布理在樂凡第剛被綁架走的時候，我們在他的房間裡設了一個紀念小壇嗎？」

「是啊……」

「我只是在想，也許他靈氣的一部分還存留在那裡。如果我們回去那裡，可能有辦法可以跟他連上線，得到一點訊息。」

「可是已經太遲了，親愛的。我們現在已經在西邊，離樂凡第很遠了。事實上，我們是在隔著沙漠的另一邊。」

「我們快到博列姆了！」馬車夫說。

所以可愛怡夫婦就繼續往博列姆前進。他們繞來繞去，終於找到了那個叫「帕比」的餐廳。他們在頭等區用餐，點了一個麻辣火鍋和蝦子。

突然，天空的顏色開始轉成暗紅色，很快地，就像被血染紅一樣。然後有火球和弓箭到處飛射，人們尖叫著逃命。可愛怡夫婦跑到外面去看究竟發生了什麼事。

竟然是阿努比斯！他上次和克喜、艾迪亞他們爭鬥的時候並沒有死，他消失後跑到博列姆這裡躲起來。

「快進來這裡面！」馬車夫叫著說。

"Oh, nothing…. Orei, you remember when we first established an altar for Bri-Bri in his bedroom after he went missing in La Frontier?"

"Yeah…."

"It's just that, I think maybe a part of Bri-Bri's soul is still there, so we might be able to communicate with him if we go there."

"It's too late though, honey. We are already in the west and so far away from La Frontier. Actually, we're on the opposite side of La Frontier across the desert."

"We're nearing Blem," the carriage driver said.

So Mr. and Mrs. Kawaii continued on the path into Blem. They went through a tangle of roads, and finally arrived at the restaurant Bubbi. They dined in the first class section, where they ordered a chili hot pot and some shrimps.

Suddenly, the sky started to turn scarlet, and soon was blood-stained. Then there were fireballs and arrows flying around. People screamed and ran for their lives. Mr. and Mrs. Kawaii came out to see what was going on.

It was Anubis! He didn't die last time in the battle with Chrishie and Adiale. He vanished to Blem to hide.

"Get in here!" shouted the carriage driver.

「不行！是阿努比斯！我們要去看布理布理是不是跟他在一起！」

阿努比斯是來劫財的，目標就是富有的可愛怡夫婦。他很貪財，這就是為什麼他總是攻擊那些經過「阿努比斯之臉」的旅客。阿努比斯很輕易地就搶走了可愛怡夫婦身上所有的錢。

阿努比斯扛著錢袋，在離開之前拋給他們一句話：

「對了！布理布理早已不在我這裡了。」

"No! It's Anubis! We have to see if Bri-Bri is with him!"

Anubis was after Kawaii family's money. He was greedy, that's why he attacked travelers that passed the desert in the Face of Anubis. Anubis easily robbed all the money that the Kawaii's have on them.

Anubis said one last thing before he left with bags of money,

"By the way, Bri-Bri is no longer with me."

第十五章 小道消息

　　因為可愛怡夫婦的錢都被搶走了，馬車夫就離開不幹了。因此他們決定走路到最近的銀行去領錢。他們到了銀行，排隊等著櫃臺服務的人很多，當他們在排隊的時候，無意間聽到幾個人在談論一群旅行者的事蹟。

　　「......那個有一頭怒髮衝冠的男生，他有一個長得很奇怪的機器，看起來好像很神奇。」

　　「你有沒有注意到一對有趣的情侶？有一個好像什麼都知道的男生，他總是跟在一個有藍色頭髮的漂亮女生旁邊。」

　　「喔，我比較記得的是另一個女生，她的脾氣很不好。和她相反的，有一個活潑開心的小男孩，眼睛大大的，他唱那個蘋果歌謠時超級可愛的！他甚至還一邊唱一邊跳舞。」

　　可愛怡太太全身都僵住了，她知道那就是愛吃蘋果的布理布理。

　　「在樂凡第看到這一群人帶給我難忘的回憶。」

Chapter XV A Gossip

Mr. and Mrs. Kawaii's horse carriage driver quit since they didn't have any money. So they walked to the nearest bank. It was about a mile away. When they got to the bank, there was a long line of people waiting for the teller's services. While waiting in the line, they overheard a few people talking about a group of travelers.

".... That boy with spiky hair, he carried a weird-looking machine that seemed very magical."

"Did you notice an interesting couple? A know-it-all boy who was always by the side of a pretty girl with blue hair."

"Oh, I remember more about another girl who had a severe temper problem. On the contrary, there was a little jolly boy with big round eyes. He was so cute when he chanted some rhyme about apples. He even danced with it!"

Mrs. Kawaii froze. She knew it must be Bri-Bri who loved apples so much.

"The sighting of that group in La Frontier brought me an unforgettable memory."

可愛怡太太很信任她的直覺，她跟可愛怡先生小聲地說：

「我知道我們下一個目的地是哪裡了！」

可愛怡先生盯著她看，他也聽到這些對話了。

「樂凡第。」他說。

可愛怡太太點點頭。

「但是要去那裡很難。距離實在太遠了，還得跨越『阿努比斯之臉』的沙漠區。」可愛怡先生聽起來憂心忡忡。

「我們可以用最快的交通工具啊！」可愛怡太太不肯放棄。

「飛機？」

「噴射機？」

「私人噴射機？」

「好！」

「我們現在就去！」

可愛怡先生從銀行帳戶裡領出了一百億元。然後他們匆匆趕往機場，租了一架噴射飛機，再雇用一個飛機駕駛員，馬上動身前往樂凡第。他們哪知道，此刻布理布理其實正在幾千英哩以外的勁剋司！

Mrs. Kawaii trusted her hunch. She whispered to Mr. Kawaii,

"I know where our next destination is."

Mr. Kawaii looked at her. He had overheard the same conversation as well.

"La Frontier," he said.

Mrs. Kawaii nodded her head.

"But it's hard to get there now. It's such a long way, all the way across the Face of Anubis," Mr. Kawaii sounded concerned.

"Let's use the fastest transportation," Mrs. Kawaii would not give in.

"Plane?"

"Jet?"

"Private jet?"

"Okay!"

"Let's go get one RIGHT NOW!"

Mr. Kawaii withdrew 10 billion dollars from his bank account. Then they rushed to the airport, rented a private jet, and hired a pilot, then set off heading towards La Frontier immediately. How could they know that Bri-Bri was actually in Zinx at that moment, which was thousands and thousands of miles away?!

　　他們飛了五個小時才到樂凡第。他們租了一台計程車，前往那座漂浮的島嶼，「可愛怡之島」。這就是可愛怡族人以前在樂凡第居住的地方。三年過去了，現在它已是個被遺棄的荒城——房子都佈滿蜘蛛網跟爛掉的木頭，草坪上雜草叢生，野草跟人一樣高，泥巴跟厚厚的灰塵完全覆蓋了道路。很難想像以前這裡曾經有過的繁華風光。

　　可愛怡太太立刻跑向那棵可愛怡大樹，可愛怡先生在後面慢慢地走著。這裡並沒有任何旅行者的跡象。但是在他們舊家裡面，那個為布理布理而築的紀念小壇，正在等著他們。

They flew for five hours to get to La Frontier. They rented a taxi to bring them to the floating island, "Island of Kawaii". This was where Kawaii people used to live in La Frontier. It's been three years, and all was abandoned now. There were houses with cobwebs and rotting wood. The lawns were overgrowing with reeds that were as tall as people. Dirt was overpowering the roads. It's hard to imagine how prosperous and glamorous it used to be in the past.

Mrs. Kawaii rushed to the Kawaii Tree. Mr. Kawaii walked slowly behind. There was no sign of the travelers. But the remains of Bri-Bri's altar in their old house were awaiting.

第十六章 消失的聲音

　　將安打開門。所有的人都在裡面，但是氣氛有點不對勁。迷蝶用她的手揉搓著自己的喉嚨，好像在掙扎什麼，她的嘴巴在動，卻沒有聲音出來。潔兒默默地坐著，她的臉色蒼白，一付很擔心的樣子。艾迪亞看起來像是在很生氣地尖叫，但是將安卻沒有聽到任何聲音。一開始將安還以為自己的耳朵有問題，直到他聽到男孩子們的對話。

　　「搞什麼鬼啊？！」克喜有點焦慮。

　　「你也看到了，女生們無法說話。」蝦肉說。

　　「對，但是為什麼？而且為什麼只有女生？」真要昇問。

　　「嗯嗯……」老人戴天尼喃喃應和。

　　「我覺得一定是在晚上的時候發生了什麼事情……」蝦肉陷入沉思。

　　「這是一種病嗎？我好害怕。」阿米慌亂起來。

　　「蘋果！蘋果！跳個曼波！喂！將安來了！他在這裡可以幫我們搞清楚到底發生了什麼事。」布理布理說著，仍然精神奕奕。

Chapter XVI Stolen Voices

John opened the door. The whole group was there, though something unusual seemed to be happening. Misty was struggling with her hands as they were rubbing at her throat. Her mouth was moving, but no sound came out. Jade was sitting there quietly, but her face was pale and she looked worried. Adiale looked like she was screaming and really upset, but John couldn't hear anything. At first John thought there was something wrong with his ears, until he heard the boys talking.

"What the heck is going on?" Chrishie was a bit anxious.

"As you can tell, the girls can't talk," said Sharo.

"Yes, but why? And why only the girls?" asked TruEthan.

"Eh?" Derteinium chirped.

"I wonder what happened during the night…," Sharo sank into a contemplation.

"Is this a disease? I'm so scared." Armi was panicking.

"Apple! Apple! Dance and ripple! Guys, John is right here to help us figure this out," said Bri-Bri, still in good spirits.

「是嗎？」所有的人都回頭。

「哈囉！朋友們！」將安很好奇，「發生什麼事了？」

「女生們通通不能說話了！我們醒來之後才發現的。一定是晚上我們睡覺的時候發生的事情。」克喜回答。

迷蝶的嘴巴動了動，說了些什麼。

「站在這裡是不能解決問題的，我們必須來調查一下。」將安說著，隨後噗嗤一聲笑出來。「但老實說我還滿高興艾迪亞不能說話的，因為我受夠了她的大嗓門，總是讓我的耳朵發疼。」

艾迪亞的臉脹紅起來，她聽到將安說的話氣得要死。她很激動地說了些什麼，但沒有人瞭解她在說什麼。

白痴將安！我希望不能講話的是你！為什麼我不能發出聲音啊？！太不公平了！艾迪亞無聲地吶喊著。

「你們怎麼知道她們不是因為從桌子上跌下來，然後摔壞了她們的聲帶？」阿米問。

「讓我們來找一些線索吧！還有，搞清楚到底為什麼只有發生在女生身上。」蝦肉說。

當男生們在搜尋線索時，阿米在窗台旁邊發現了一塊可疑的碎布。

"Really?" everyone turned around.

"Hello friends!" John was curious, "What happened?"

"The girls can't talk. We just found out when we woke up. It must be something during the night while we were sleeping," said Chrishie.

Misty mouthed something.

"Standing around isn't going to work. We have to investigate," John said, followed by a chuckle. "But honestly I'm glad that Adiale can't talk because I'm tired of hearing her screaming. It always hurts my ears."

Adiale's face turned red. She was angry when she heard this. She mouthed something agitatedly that nobody could understand.

Idiot John! I wish it was you who lost the voice! Why am I unable to make any sounds? It's not fair! Adiale was shouting silently.

"How do you know they didn't just fall off a table and break their vocal cords?" asked Armi.

"Let's see if we can find some clues. Also, figure out why only the *girls* can't talk," said Sharo.

When the boys went searching for clues, Armi found something suspicious, a bit of cloth stuck at the window.

第十七章 給女孩們的詛咒

　　為什麼這裡會有一塊碎布？將安思忖著。這個核電廠已經廢棄很久了。

　　將安把它拿起來，仔細地檢視著。這塊布是絨布的材質，顯然很舊，至少有十幾年了。還有，它的花紋看來像是女生衣服上的。

　　「喂！來看！」將安叫著，並把他關於這塊布的年代及花紋的觀察講給大家聽。

　　「這塊布很不尋常，一定藏有什麼祕密，可以幫助我們找到答案。」將安說。

　　「確定嗎？」克喜質疑。

　　「我很確定！這是一個重要的線索。」將安斬釘截鐵地說，把這塊布放進自己的口袋裡。

　　「好吧!」克喜聳聳肩。「對了，我在想，不知道那個怪物是不是還在外面。」

　　「好像不在了。我剛剛去窗台外面拿那塊布的時候順便瞄了一眼。」將安說。

Chapter XVII A Curse for Girls

Why is there a piece of cloth here? thought John. *The nuclear power plant has been abandoned for years.*

John grabbed it and examined it closely. The cloth was velvet and obviously very old, at least from decades ago. Also it had patterns that were most likely from a women's dress.

"Hey! Peeps!" John shouted, then he shared his observations with others.

"This piece of cloth is unusual. It may hide something we don't know — that will help us," said John.

"Sure?" asked Chrishie.

"Yes, I'm sure. This cloth is important," John confirmed. He put that piece of cloth in his pocket.

"Fine," Chrishie shrugged. "By the way, I wonder if the monster is still out there."

"It doesn't seem like it. I just peeked when I grabbed that piece of cloth from outside," said John.

「但是，仍然有 13.2745%的機率那個怪物還在附近。如果它還在的話，應該會是在南邊或西邊的出口那裡。」將安看著手上剛剛拆下來的地圖，指著那兩個門口。

「為什麼？」真要昇問。

「因為我們是從建築物北邊的煙囪進來的。而建築物的東邊有一個湖，記得嗎？我們站在平台上眺望的時候看到的。」將安解釋。

「好，那就是說，我們應該從北邊出去？」克喜轉向蝦肉，徵詢他的意見，因為蝦肉是一個很有遠見的人。

蝦肉也同意。

「那我們走吧！」布理布理說，跟平常一樣無憂無慮。

他們往北邊的門口走去。當他們來到外面，一切都很通暢，沒有怪物的蹤跡，除了之前被它拆毀的平台碎片散落一地。

他們很安全地離開了核電廠。走了一段路，來到了一個叢林前面，那裡豎立了一塊牌子，上面寫著說：

"However, there is a 13.2754% chance that the monster is still here. If he is, he should be around either the south gate or the west gate," John looked at the map in his hand and pointed to those two gates.

"Why?" asked TruEthan.

"Because we came in from the chimney that was on the north side of the building, and the east side is a lake, remember? We saw that when we were looking out on the deck," John explained.

"Ok, then maybe we should exit from the north gate?" Chrishie turned to Sharo looking for his advice because Sharo was very visionary and good at big pictures. Sharo agreed.

"Then let's go!" said Bri-Bri. He was carefree as usual.

They headed to the north gate. When they came outside, it was all clear. There was no sign of the monster, except for the dismantled pieces of the deck from yesterday.

They made it, leaving the building safely. They walked for a while and found themselves at the front of a jungle. There was a wooden sign. It said:

　　「小心！！！千萬不要到勁剋司的核電廠裡
面去！尤其是女生！因為一個詛咒會讓妳失去妳
的聲音！以前已經發生過很多次了！有一個短暫
的解藥可以讓妳恢復聲音，但只有兩個小時，那
就是吃一朵紫羅蘭花。」

　　「一個詛咒……原來如此。」克喜說。

　　艾迪亞的眼睛睜得老大，張開嘴說了些話。阿米盯著
她的嘴，很仔細地看，試著解讀，然後他說：

　　「我想艾迪亞在問的是：我們要到哪裡去找紫羅蘭
花？」

"CAUTIOUN!!! DO NOT GO IN THE POWER PLANT OF ZINX, ESPECIALLY IF YOU ARE A GIRL! YOU WILL LOSE YOUR VOICE BECAUSE OF A CURSE! THIS HAS HAPPENED MANY TIMES BEFORE! THERE IS A TEMPORARY CURE THAT YOU CAN REGAIN YOUR VOICE FOR TWO HOURS — EAT A VIOLET FLOWER."

"A curse…, that's why," said Chrishie.

Adiale's eyes were wide open and then mouthed something. Armi looked at her closely and said:

"I think Adiale is asking, where can we find flowers of violet?"

第十八章 # 分道揚鑣

　　潔兒的嘴巴在動。阿米現在開始能讀懂一些唇語了，他滿有天分的。他翻譯說：

　　「我和迷蝶有一個叔叔住在因努那個跳越區，他很懂園藝，知道很多花的知識。也許他可以告訴我們到哪裡去找紫羅蘭花！」

　　她想到這個主意覺得很興奮，迷蝶也開心地點著頭。艾迪亞稍稍鬆了一口氣，巴不得能盡快出發。

　　「太好了！」克喜說。「我們就去幫妳們找解藥吧！雖然只是暫時的解藥。」

　　「等等——我覺得我們應該先去找若薇亞公主。」眞要昇說。

　　「爲什麼？」克喜問。

　　「她現在被強柯囚禁著，我擔心她的安全。」

　　「她是一個鬼魂，沒什麼可以傷害她的。」

　　「我很想念她……」眞要昇低聲咕噥。

Chapter XVIII **The Split**

Jade mouthed something. Armi was really good at knowing what people were mouthing. He interpreted what Jade said,

"Misty and I have an uncle that lives in Yinu. He knows a lot about flowers and gardening. He would probably know where to find violets!"

She was excited about this idea. Misty also nodded her head, very happily. Adiale felt so relieved and could not wait to leave as soon as possible.

"Great!" said Chrishie. "Let's go find the solution for your voices, though it's just a temporary one."

"Wait — I think we should find Princess Rovia first," TruEthan said.

"Why?" Chrishie asked.

"I'm concerned about her being prisoned by Jrunk," answered TruEthan.

"She's a ghost. Nothing can harm her," Chrishie responded.

"And I miss her…," TruEthan murmured.

「這些女生也很想念她們的聲音啊！」克喜說。

「我要找若薇亞公主！她是幫我找到家人的嚮導。」布理布理說。

「我也贊成先找若薇亞公主。」蝦肉說。「反正我們都已經在這裡了。艾迪亞，你是可愛怡家族的拯救者，我想即使沒有聲音，妳也還是可以做到的。」

艾迪亞顯得很不高興，她動嘴作無聲的抗議。

大家繼續爭辯了好一會兒，有人覺得應該繼續去找若薇亞公主，有人覺得應該先去幫女生們找解藥。

「乾脆我們分成兩隊好了！」將安建議。「每一隊有各自的任務，等到我們完成目前的緊急任務之後，就再碰頭，然後一起去找布理布理的家人。」

大家彼此對看，覺得這似乎是個不錯的辦法。

終於，每個人都同意分組進行。跟著眞要昇的這一組有眞要昇自己，布理布理，蝦肉，跟將安。跟著克喜的這一組有克喜自己，阿米，老人戴天尼，艾迪亞，迷蝶，和潔兒。

"The girls miss their voices, too!" said Chrishie.

"I want Princess Rovia! She is the guide to find my Family!" Bri-Bri said.

"I'm on the side of finding Princess Rovia, too," said Sharo. "Since we are already here. Adiale, you are the savior of the Kawaii family. I think you can do it even without your voice."

Adiale apparently was unhappy, she mouthed something in protest.

People continued their debate about whether they should continue to find Princess Rovia first or find a cure for the girls.

"How about we split in two groups?" John suggested. "Each group has its own mission. We can meet again after we complete the urgent missions, then go find Bri-Bri's family together."

They looked at one another. It did sound like a good idea.

Finally, everyone agreed on the split. On TruEthan's group, there were TruEthan, Bri-Bri, Sharo, and John. Chrishie's group had Chrishie, Armi, Derteinium, Adiale, Misty, and Jade.

　　「但是，我們要怎麼出去呢？」克喜突然想起來他們沒辦法穿透在勁剋司外圍的鬼牆。「只有真要昇的『靈魂之風』可以帶我們離開這裡，不是嗎？」

　　「還有另一個法力，是專門逃脫用的。」老人戴天尼說。「叫做『跑酷』。」

　　「我想阿米很適合來啓動這個法力。」老人戴天尼看著阿米。

　　「我？」阿米很驚喜被選中。

　　「雖然我知道這些所有的招式，但是這些法力只能被從地球來的小孩施展才會有效，大人或是佛夢達裡面的人是沒辦法用的。」

　　於是老人戴天尼開始示範動作。他向前走了三步，原地轉 180 度，然後單腳跳了兩下。

　　阿米跟著他照做，一個跑酷的方塊物就突然憑空出現了。克喜這一組的人紛紛跳上去那個方塊物。

　　克喜等到最後，他有點感傷。他和真要昇是最好的朋友，自從來到佛夢達的世界之後，他們一直都是一起旅行的，這會是他們第一次在這段旅程上分開。真要昇也是一樣地感傷。他倆互相擁抱，祝福彼此的隊伍能有好運，也相約在完成了各自的任務之後，到樂凡第相會。

"But, how will we get out?" Chrishie suddenly remembered that they were not able to penetrate the ghost barriers around Zinx. "Only TruEthan's Wind of the Soul can bring us get out of Zinx, right?"

"There is a special power for exiting," Derteinium said. "It's a parkour."

"I think Armi will be good in this move," Derteinium looked at Armi.

"Me?" Armi was surprised, but glad.

"Even though I know all these powers, they can only be exerted by kids from the Earth, not for grown-ups or those who are part of Formonda."

Then Derteinium started demonstrating the move. He took three steps forward, pivoted 180 degrees, and then jumped single-legged twice.

Armi followed Derteinium's steps. When he did, an object for parkour appeared. Chrishie's group started to jump on the parkour object.

Chrishie waited to go last. He was feeling sad. He and TruEthan were best friends and they had been traveling together ever since they came in the world of Formonda. This would be the first time they separated in their journey. TruEthan felt the same. They hugged each other and blessed each other's group with good luck. They also made a promise that after they complete their missions, they would meet in La Frontier.

　　然後克喜轉身離開，跳上那個飄浮在空中的方塊物。這時有個東西從他的背包裡掉了出來，眞要昇從地上撿起來一看。

　　這不是我在雷電市集買的那本佛夢達的歷史書嗎？我完全忘記了！也許我可以在這本書裡面找到關於這個詛咒的線索。還有，只要一點點線索也好，告訴我心愛的若薇亞在哪裡……

Then Chrishie walked away and jumped on the blocks that were floating in midair. Something fell out of Chrishie's backpack. TruEthan picked it up from the ground.

Isn't this the history book that I bought in Thunder Market? I totally forgot about it! Maybe I can find some clues about the curse, and where, just where, my precious Rovia might be….

第十九章 強柯的傷心往事

　　傅瑞德坐在一個椅子上。他坐在一個時髦餐廳的椅子上。他跟他的妻子一起坐在一個時髦餐廳的椅子上。他們結婚快要滿兩週年了，他們住在勁剋司這個跳越區裡。有些事你必須要知道——傅瑞德就是二十年前的強柯。

　　傅瑞德在核電廠裡面工作，他是這裡的其中一個科學家。每天晚上他下班回家之後，他的妻子都會唱一首歌給他聽。她是一個職業歌手，到處表演，人們都愛慕她那優美的歌聲。她也有一個很優美的名字，叫做羅蘭。

　　傅瑞德是整個勁剋司裡最快樂的人——在工作上，他運用他的知識、好奇心、跟科學方法從事新的研究；在家裡，他有一個可愛的妻子跟他相親相愛。每個月他們會有一次到鎮上的一個高級沙龍裡，跳舞、飲酒、唱歌、談笑。他們會待到很晚，說些笑話，或對彼此表達愛意。傅瑞德願意為這樣與羅蘭永遠享受美好的生活付出任何代價。

Chapter XIX Jrunk's Sad Story

Fred was sitting on a chair. He was sitting on a chair in a fancy restaurant. He was sitting on a chair in a fancy restaurant with his wife. They got married almost 2 years ago. They lived in the Jumper Zinx. There is something you need to know about Fred — Fred was Jrunk, 20 years younger.

Fred worked at the nuclear energy plant. He was one of the scientists there. Every night when Fred came back from work, his wife would sing for him. She was a professional singer who performed publicly, people admired her for her beautiful voice. She also had a beautiful name — Violet.

Fred was the happiest man in Zinx. At work he used his knowledge, curiosity, and methods to find new ways for research. At home he had an adorable wife to love. Once a month, he and Violet would go out to a saloon for dancing, drinking, singing, and laughing. They stayed up late, they told jokes, and they expressed their love to each other. Fred would give anything just to be able to always be with Violet happily.

　　他們結婚兩週年的紀念日就快到了。他迫不及待，也希望沒有突來的工作會干擾他這一天的興致。但是他剛剛才接到通知，那一天他有個重要的實驗，因此他覺得很失望。

　　五月六號的早上，傅瑞德買了一束紫羅蘭花，還有一個蛋糕，是羅蘭最喜歡的口味，上面有她最喜歡的菓子。羅蘭很開心，她知道傅瑞德很愛她，但是她想要在這特別的一天做點什麼不一樣的。她突發奇想——在下午的時候跑去傅瑞德工作的地方給他一個驚喜！她打算偷偷溜進他的辦公室，向他丟灑五彩紙屑砲。一定會很好玩的！她的眼睛亮起來。

　　五月六號下午三點零二分，傅瑞德和他的同事們正準備好要開始他們的實驗。這是一個危險的實驗，所以他們都穿上了防護衣，以免發生不測。但是羅蘭並沒有，她在他們的爆炸實驗剛剛開始時溜進來了。傅瑞德剛好轉過身來看到她。化學物質開始滋滋作響，越來越大。傅瑞德大喊：

　　「快跑！要爆炸了！」

　　羅蘭企圖跳出窗戶外面，她的衣服被窗台卡住，撕掉一小塊，留在那裡。然後，一聲巨大的爆炸在她身後響起。她死於爆炸的衝擊力。

It was almost their two-year anniversary on May 6th. He couldn't wait. He hoped his work wasn't going to interrupt him on that day. But then he found out he had to do an important experiment that day. He was disappointed.

In the morning of May 6th, Fred bought a bunch of violets and a cake with her favorite toppings and her favorite flavors. Violet was happy, she knew how much Fred loved her. But she wanted something different on this special day. She came up with an idea to surprise Fred at work in the afternoon. She planned to sneak into his work place and throw a confetti bomb at him. *It will be so fun!* Her eyes sparkled.

3:02 pm on May 6th, Fred and his colleagues were getting ready for the experiment. It was a dangerous one, so they were wearing protective gears, just in case something might go wrong. But Violet didn't. She sneaked in when the explosion started. Fred turned around just as Violet entered. The chemicals started fizzling, it was growing bigger. Fred yelled,

"RUN!!! IT"S GONNA BLOW!!!"

Violet tried to leap out of the window. Her dress got stuck on the window sill. It ripped and a piece of cloth was left behind. Then, a big explosion was heard behind her. Violet died from the impact.

　　沒有任何語言可以描述傅瑞德的悲傷及痛苦。他開始
酗酒，越喝越多。他對人生已經失去盼望，剩下的只有憤
怒和憎恨。他開始學習黑魔法，並對核電廠施下詛咒，讓
所有進來的女孩子都失去聲音——因為他不願被提醒，想
起羅蘭那天籟般的聲音。還有，他也學會了如何駕馭黑
暗，佔領了好幾個跳越區，像是周尼波町和強柯運動（以
前曾經叫做「愛的運動」）。

　　最後，他給自己改名，叫做強柯。

There were no words to describe Fred's grief and agony. He started drinking alcohol, more and more. He had lost hope about life, all that was left for him was anger and hatred. So he started to learn dark magic. He cast a curse on the nuclear power plant that all girls staying there will lose their voices. He was trying to avoid the memory of Violet's heavenly voice. Also he learned how to harness the darkness. He took over several Jumpers, such as Juniperdinto and Jrunk Movement (which used to be called "Love Movement").

Finally, he renamed himself Jrunk.

第二十章 特別的若薇亞

「原來如此！」眞要昇說。

「我找到的那塊碎布是羅蘭的。」將安說。

「現在我們大概可以猜得到要到哪裡去找若薇亞公主
了。」蝦肉說。

「哪裡？」

「強柯的家。」

「對喔！
很有可能。」

「那我們
就去看看！」

他們循著歷史書上的線索去找強柯住的地方。他的家
位在一個被樹林環繞的小村莊裡面，那裡有餐館，沙龍，
精品店。它過去一定曾經是一個精緻可愛的小鎮，但現在
已經沒落了。強柯的房子看起來很老舊，是用石頭建造的，
上面爬滿藤蔓。

Chapter XX The Special Rovia

"So that's why!" said TruEthan.

"The piece of cloth I got was from Violet," said John.

"Now we can probably guess where we can find Princess Rovia," said Sharo.

"Where?"

"Jrunk's home."

"Ya, very likely."

"Let's go check it out then!"

They followed the clues in the book to find out where Jrunk's house was. Jrunk's house was located in a village that was surrounded by trees. There were diners, saloons, and boutiques. It must have been a nice sweet village in the past. Now it had just declined. Jrunk's house looked very old, it was built with stones and covered in vines.

他們在窗戶外面打探。強柯一個人在家喝酒,地板上散落了幾十個空酒瓶。他醉得很厲害,完全不省人事。於是他們想辦法從廁所的窗戶潛入。他們很小心地在房子裡面鬼鬼祟祟地行動,搜尋每一個房間,但是他們並沒有看到若薇亞公主。最後,眞要昇看到一雙球鞋,在一個門旁邊。

「這是若薇亞公主的球鞋!」眞要昇倒吸了一口氣。「她在雷電市集買的。」

「對!我也記得。」布理布理小聲地說。

他們打開那扇門,看到一個往下的階梯。

這一定是地下室。眞要昇想。

他們走下去。那裡又暗又冷,他們聽見機器的嗶嗶聲。當他們的眼睛能適應黑暗之後,他們看到了若薇亞公主被困在一個玻璃球狀罩裡面,是用鬼牆的材質做的。在那個玻璃罩子外面有一些電線,連接到許多的機器上。

當若薇亞公主看到眞要昇時,她的眼睛張得好大。她很驚訝,但也很高興。她把雙手放在玻璃罩上面,滿心期待著。眞要昇趕緊跑過去,跟她說:

「不用擔心!強柯現在醉得不省人事,我們有足夠的時間可以把妳救出來。」

They spied outside the window. Jrunk was alone, drinking alcohol. Dozens of bottles were scattered on the floor. He was very drunk and completely unconscious. They managed to enter through the window of a bathroom and carefully sneaked around the house searching room by room, but they didn't find Princess Rovia. Finally, TruEthan saw a pair of sneakers next to a door.

"Princess Rovia's sneakers!" TruEthan gasped. "She bought them when we were in the Thunder Market."

"Yes! I remember them, too," whispered Bri-Bri.

They opened the door to find a flight of stairs going down.

This must be the basement, thought TruEthan.

They walked down. It was dark and cold. They heard beeping from machines. When their eyes adapted to the darkness, they saw Princess Rovia being confined in a glass globe that's made of ghost barrier. There were lots of machines around the globe, with cables connecting to it.

When Princess Rovia saw TruEthan, her eyes grew wide. She was in shock, but happy. She put her hands on the glass looking forward. TruEthan's rushed to the globe and said:

"No worries! Jrunk is very drunk at the moment. We should have enough time to get you out of here."

「但是我們要怎樣讓她從玻璃罩裡面出來？」布理布理問。

他們開始努力嘗試各種辦法來控制那些機器，試著要打開玻璃罩。將安最後按下一個按鈕，成功地讓玻璃罩自動分成兩半打開，若薇亞公主終於可以出來。

他們轉向地下室的門口，確認一切都很安全，很快地跑上階梯。強柯還是不省人事。他們從窗戶逃出來，當他們終於遠離強柯的房子之後，才鬆了一口氣。

眞要昇有很多問題想問若薇亞公主，但是蝦肉說：

「別急，我們必須先趕快走得越遠越好，以免強柯等一下醒過來追趕我們。」

「眞要昇，快！用你的法力帶我們離開勁剋司！」布理布理催著他。

於是眞要昇施展「靈魂之風」的法力，他們就騎著那股魔法的風，離開了勁剋司。

「所以，到底發生了什麼事？」眞要昇問若薇亞公主。

「我後來才知道，強柯一開始之所以要殺我是因爲他很嫉妒我們。」若薇亞公主指的是在他們在可愛怡聖壇遭到黑暗攻擊的那一天晚上。「他嫉妒所有相愛的情侶，因爲他會想起發生在他身上的事，就忿忿不平。他以前曾經深愛一個女人，她的名字好像是羅蘭……」

"But how are we going to get her out of that globe?" Bri-Bri asked.

The group worked hard trying to figure out how to control those machines in order to open the globe. John finally made it to push a button that split the globe so that Princess Rovia could exit.

They turned towards the door. Coast was clear. They quickly ran up the stairs. Jrunk was still unconscious. They escaped through the window and when they got far away from Jrunk's mansion, they were relieved.

TruEthan had so many questions that he wanted to ask Princess Rovia. But Sharo said:

"Before that, we should leave here as quickly as possible, just in case Jrunk might wake up anytime soon."

"Quick! TruEthan. Use your power and take us away from Zinx!" Bri-Bri hurried him.

So TruEthan initiated the Wind of the Soul. They rode in the magic wind and were on the way out.

"So what's happened?" TruEthan asked Prince Rovia.

"I realized that Jrunk wanted me dead in the first place because he was jealous of us." Princess Rovia was referring to Junk's darkness attack when they were in Kawaii Altar. "He is jealous of couples that are in love. He thought it wasn't fair, what had happened to him. He used to be in love with a woman, I think her name was Violet...."

「是的，我們知道羅蘭的事。我們從歷史書上看到這一段過去的事蹟。」眞要昇說。

「喔！好。後來強柯很驚訝我變成一個鬼魂。他很好奇爲什麼我死了之後仍在這裡，而羅蘭卻消失了。他想知道爲什麼，所以他想，如果可以用我來做實驗，找到答案，也許他就可以把羅蘭帶回來。他以前是個科學家。」

「啊！這樣聽起來很有道理。」蝦肉說。

「不過強柯的確問了一個很好的問題——爲什麼妳還在這裡而羅蘭不行？妳到底有什麼特別之處？」將安問。

"Yes, we know about Violet. We learned about his past from the history book," TruEthan said.

"Oh, okay. Then Jrunk was surprised that I'm still around as a ghost. He was wondering how come I could still be here as a ghost but not Violet after her death. He wants to know why, and thinks maybe he can bring Violet back as a ghost, if he can work it out by examining me and doing some experiments on me. He used to be a scientist."

"Ahh, now it makes more sense," Sharo said.

"He indeed has a valid question though — why are you still around but not Violet? What's special about you?" John asked.

第二十一章 紫羅蘭與眼淚

　　克喜他們跑酷了一整天，精疲力竭。當他們坐在一個大方塊上休息時，有一架飛機經過。飛行員看到他們，就飛下來，在此降落。

　　「嗨！」飛行員說。

　　「嗨！很高興在這裡碰到你！你可以載我們去因努嗎？」克喜問。

　　「當然可以！」飛行員說，「上來吧！」

　　他們爬上登機的梯子。這是一架頭等艙的飛機，看起來像是私人噴射機。

　　「你從哪裡飛來？」克喜問。

　　「樂凡第。我帶一對夫婦到那裡去，他們看起來好像急著在找什麼人。」

　　「喔……你以前去過因努嗎？」克喜問。

　　「有啊！我去過佛夢達的每一個跳越區。」飛行員回答。「你們去因努做什麼？」

Chapter XXI **Violets and Tears**

Chrishie's group had been parkouring for a day. They were all exhausted. While they were taking a break on a big square, a plane flew by. The pilot saw them, then flew down and landed.

"Hi," he said.

"Hi, it's good to see you here! Can you help us get to Yinu?" asked Chrishie.

"Sure!" said the pilot. "Come aboard!"

They climbed the stairs into the plane. It was a first class plane. It looked like a private jet — it probably was.

"Where are you flying from?" asked Chrishie.

"La Frontier. I took a couple there. They looked like they were in a hurry looking for someone."

"Oh… Have you ever been to Yinu?"

"Yes, I have. I've been to every Jumper in Formonda," answered the pilot. "Why do you need to go to Yinu?"

　　克喜告訴他有關他們進到勁剋司的核電廠裡面，及女生們失去聲音的事。

　　「你知道這個給女生的詛咒嗎？」克喜問。

　　「我知道。以前有一個人叫傅瑞德……」

　　接下來他就告訴他們你在前兩章讀到的那個故事。

　　「哦！原來如此！」阿米，還有其他每一個人都這樣反應，包括那些不能說話的女生。

　　「我們快到了！扣上你們的安全帶。」飛行員說。

　　他們很迅速地降落在因努。因努是一個在山上的跳越區，山的名字叫做因努濤　（簡稱因努）。它隔壁有另一個跳越區，納威口。納威口是一個山谷，而因努是一座山。這兩個跳越區都是開滿花的地方，而且有很多著名的自然風景區景點，像是因努季村，瓦堤落，費奴山，底居河，哈里科塔森林，和琉霧湖。

　　他們跟著潔兒和迷蝶穿過因努季村。她們在一個小茅舍前面停下來，然後搖響掛在門前的一個風鈴。門很快地打開，站著一個高大的男人，臉上掛著友善的微笑。

　　「潔兒！迷蝶！真高興看到妳們！」

　　迷蝶上前去擁抱她的叔叔時，嘴巴還一邊在說些什麼。

Chrishie told him about how they went into the nuclear power plant in Zinx and the girls lost their voices.

"Do you know about the curse that makes girls lose their voice?" asked Chrishie.

"Oh, yeah. There was this guy called Fred…."

He went over what you read in *Jrunk's sad story*.

"Oh! That's why!" responded Armi, so did everyone else in the group, including the silent girls.

"We're almost at Yinu, buckle your seatbelt," said the pilot.

They landed swiftly in Yinu. Yinu was a Jumper on a mountain called Yīnutoù (Yinu for short). Another Jumper, Nawico, was bordering Yinu. Nawico was a valley and Yinu was a mountain. Both Yinu and Nawaico were flowering Jumpers. There were some famous vista points in these two Jumpers like Yinuji Village, Watilo Point, Mt. Feinu, Diju River, Haricotta Forest, and Ryowu Lake.

They followed Jade and Misty through Yinuji Village. Finally, Jade and Misty stopped in front of a little hut. They rang a chime that was hung outside the door. The door flew open and there stood a big man with a friendly smile.

"Jade! Misty! How good to see you!"

Misty mouthed something while she went up to hug her uncle.

「這些人是誰啊？」他注意到其他幾個陌生人。

「很抱歉打擾你，先生。」克喜說，「但是你的兩個姪女都不能說話，有一個詛咒讓她們變成這樣，失去聲音。我們是她們的朋友，要幫她們找紫羅蘭花作為解藥。」

「紫羅蘭花……我們已經很久很久沒有再看過紫羅蘭花了！我想你們大概在佛夢達的任何一個地方都不會找得到的。」

每個人都像被打敗一樣，很沮喪。潔兒和迷蝶無力地坐倒在地上。

「但是，我倒是知道一個魔法可以讓它開花。」叔叔一邊把她們兩個扶起來，一邊說。「你們必須用眼淚來澆灌一棵小樹苗……」

「哦！我有一棵小樹苗！」老人戴天尼很興奮。

艾迪亞說了些什麼。阿米幫她翻譯：

「艾迪亞說她想試試看。」

老人戴天尼把那棵他在雷電市集買的小樹苗交給艾迪亞。艾迪亞很努力想一些傷心的事。終於，一顆小小的淚珠從她的臉上流下來，落在樹苗上面。

什麼也沒發生。

眾人都很困惑。艾迪亞的表情很生氣。

"Who are these people?" he noticed the strangers in the group.

"Sorry to interrupt," said Chrishie. "But your two nieces can't talk. There was a curse that made them silent. They lost their voices. We are their friends, trying to help them by finding violets as a cure."

"Violets…. We have lost the flowers of violet for many, many years. I don't think you can find them anywhere in Formonda anymore."

Everyone was dismayed. Jade and Misty sat down on the floor, feebly.

"But, I do know a magic way to make it flower," he picked up his nieces. "You need to water a sapling with tears."

"Oh, I have a sapling!" Derteinium was excited.

Adiale mouthed something.

"Adiale said she wants to try it out," said Armi.

Derteinium gave Adiale his sapling, the one he bought in the Thunder Market. Adiale tried very hard to think about some sad things. Finally, a single drop of tears came down her face, then fell on the sapling.

Nothing happened.

People were confused. Adiale made an angry face.

「你們沒讓我把話說完。」叔叔嘆了一口氣。「不是任何眼淚都可以，一定要是歡喜的眼淚。」

「歡喜的眼淚？」大家齊聲說。

"You didn't let me finish," sighed the uncle. "It's not any tears. It must be *tears of joy.*"

"Tears of joy?" said everyone.

第二十二章 3-D 列印的洋娃娃

　　可愛怡先生腳步沉重地跟在可愛怡太太身後，來到布理布理的房間。他們進來之後，看到一個機器，正在製作一個東西。他們靠近一看，發現那是一個 3D 列印機。

　　這是一個很厲害的 3D 列印機，可以同時印出很多顏色。你可能以爲它沒什麼了不起，但這個很特別，因爲它就是之前布理布理在雷電市集買的，然後丟進蟲洞裡面的那一個。

　　這個 3D 列印機剛剛才印完一個洋娃娃，大約是一支筆的大小。這個洋娃娃有藍色的頭髮，發出金光，穿著一件白色的長袍及一雙球鞋。可愛怡夫婦看著這個洋娃娃，但不知道這對他們找到布理布理有什麼幫助。他們左看右看，注意到在它穿的球鞋底部，印著一行小字：

　　「製於芬溪」

　　他們於是決定到芬溪這個跳越區去，這是目前唯一的一個線索了。他們找了另一個飛機駕駛員帶他們去芬溪。

Chapter XXII The 3-D Printed Doll

Mr. Kawaii trudged after Mrs. Kawaii into Bri-Bri's bedroom. When they got in, they saw a machine making something. They got closer and figured it was a 3-D printer.

It was a super 3-D printer that could print multiple colors. You might think this was pretty ordinary, but this one was magical. It was the one that Bri-Bri bought back in Thunder Market and threw into the wormhole.

The 3-D printer had just finished printing a doll, the size of a pen. It had blue hair with a golden glow, wearing a white gown and a pair of sneakers. Mr. and Mrs. Kawaii looked at this doll but had no idea what connection it might have to help them finding Bri-Bri. They examined it closely, and noticed that in the bottom of the sneakers, it wrote,

"Made In Fancī"

They decided to go to Fancī. That's the only clue they had for now. They called in another pilot to fly them to Fancī.

　　芬溪很像巴黎，是一個很羅曼蒂克的城市。情侶們會來這裡的河上搖槳划船，繁忙的街道上有許多賣衣服及裝飾品的店鋪，有流行時尚的，也有異國情調的東西。每個角落都有咖啡店，空氣中充滿了咖啡及烘焙麵包的香味。

　　他們抵達之後，第一件事就是去找下榻的飯店。他們來到全城最棒的酒店，「菱鏡之光大酒店」。它長得就像一個巨大的三菱鏡一樣，透明、多稜角、且閃耀著反射的光芒。他們跟櫃臺的接待員稍微聊了一下。

　　「你知道哪裡有在做洋娃娃的嗎？」可愛怡太太問。

　　「不知道，夫人。」櫃臺小姐回答。

　　「那做球鞋的呢？像這一雙一樣。」她繼續問，把那個洋娃娃拿出來給櫃臺小姐看，指著洋娃娃腳上的鞋子。

　　「我想不出來。但是這裡有一條街專門賣各式各樣的鞋子，叫做阿瘦街，你也許可以到那裡去找找看。」

　　「太好了！謝謝你提供的資訊。」

　　但是這資訊並沒有什麼幫助。可愛怡夫婦花了好幾天在街上跟店裡搜尋，尤其是鞋子店，但是一無所獲。

Fancī was like Paris, a very romantic Jumper. Couples would come here to row a boat on the river. It had busy streets with shops for apparel, both fashion designs and exotic stuff. Cafés were in every street corner and the air was filled with nice aromas of coffee and bakeries.

After they arrived, the first thing they did was to find somewhere to stay. They checked into the fanciest hotel in town, the Prism Hotel. It looked like a gigantic prism — transparent, multiple-angled, and shinning with reflected lights. They had a little talk with the front desk receptionist.

"Do you know any place that makes dolls?" asked Mrs. Kawaii.

"No, madam," said the front desk lady.

"Or any place that makes sneakers like this?" she followed up, showing her the doll and pointing to the sneakers on its feet.

"I don't think so. But there is a special street selling all kinds of shoes. It is called Asoeh Street. You may want to check it out there."

"Great! Thank you for the information," said Mrs. Kawaii.

It was not very useful anyway. They spent days searching in shops, especially for those sneakers, but did not find anything.

　　有一天，他們回到酒店之後，在回房間的路上，他們正在討論怎樣把這個洋娃娃跟鑰匙圈連在一起，這樣比較容易攜帶，也比較安全。當他們在上樓梯的時候，有一個年輕人正在往下走。可愛怡太太沒注意看，不小心撞到他，手上的洋娃娃和鑰匙圈掉到階梯地毯上。那個年輕人把它們撿起來，瞥了一眼之後，很驚訝地說：

　　「這跟我妹妹長得一模一樣！自從波理斯瑪被摧毀之後她就失蹤了。你們是怎麼會有這個洋娃娃的？」年輕人問。

　　「你的妹妹？喔，我們不認識她。我們是在找我們失蹤的兒子時得到這個洋娃娃的。我們一直想從這個洋娃娃身上找到一些線索，因為我們相信它可以帶我們找到我們兒子。所以你妹妹也失蹤了？」可愛怡先生問。

　　「是的。但老實說，我不確定她是否仍然活著……」他有點傷心。「波理斯瑪被摧毀之後我就到這裡來找一個朋友。」

　　「我的名字是歐瑞，這是我太太，梅莉。我們的孩子布理布理已經失蹤三年了，我們正在努力搜索他的下落。」可愛怡先生解釋。「或許我們注定要碰到一起的，畢竟那個在我兒子房間裡神奇出現的 3D 列印機印出了這個洋娃娃給我們。所以它一定帶著重要的信息——透過你妹妹，我們可以找到布理布理。」

One day, after they returned to the hotel, as they walked back to their room, they were discussing about putting the doll on a keychain so it's easier and safer to carry it around. When they climbed up the stairs, a young man was going down. By accident Mrs. Kawaii bumped into him without looking. The doll and the keychain fell on the carpet of the staircase. The young man picked them up, he was surprised when he glanced the doll.

"This is an image of my sister! She has been missing ever since Purisima was destroyed. How did you get this doll?" the young man asked.

"Your sister? Oh, we don't know her. We got this while searching for our missing son. We have been trying to figure out more clues from this doll because we believe it could lead us to find our son. So your sister is missing, too?" Mr. Kawaii answered.

"Yes. But honestly, I'm not even sure if she is still alive…," he looked sad. "I came here to find a friend after I learned that Purisima had been destroyed."

"My name is Orei, and this is my wife, Melli. Our child, Bri-Bri, has been missing for 3 years. We're on a quest to find him," Mr. Kawaii explained. "Maybe we're meant to search together. After all, the 3-D printer that magically appeared in my son's room printed this doll for us. So it must carry an important message that Bri-Bri somehow can be found through your sister."

　　「有意思……好的！我很願意加入你們，或許我會
有機會再見到我的妹妹！」他開始覺得有希望。

　　「對了，我叫卡爾，波理斯瑪的卡爾王子。」他說。
「我妹妹是若薇亞公主。」

"Interesting…. Yes! I'd love to join you on the quest. Maybe I will get to see my sister again!" he started to feel some hope.

"By the way, I am Kale, Prince Kale of Purisima," he said. "And my sister's name is Princess Rovia."

第二十三章 # 可愛怡聖壇的客棧

　　可愛怡夫婦和卡爾王子決定先回到可愛怡聖壇去商討計策。可愛怡太太突然有個主意：

　　「要不我們先去可愛怡聖壇和林特魁司的邊界那裡去？看看我留給布理布理的戒指和紙卷是否仍在那裡。」

　　「這樣也好。」可愛怡先生說。

　　可愛怡先生向卡爾王子解釋關於之前他們留下戒指和紙卷的事。於是他們買了頭等艙的機票，飛到了林特魁司國際機場，然後租了一輛車，直接開往邊界的地方。

　　可愛怡太太之前留在那個漩渦入口裡面的東西已經不在了。

　　「不見了！」可愛怡太太叫著說。

　　「戒指和紙卷都不見了嗎？」可愛怡先生問。

　　「對！兩個都不見了！」

　　「嗯......」可愛怡先生陷入沉思。

Chapter XXIII The Inn at Kawaii Altar

Mr. Kawaii, Mrs. Kawaii, and Prince Kale decided to first go back to Kawaii Altar to make a plan. Then, Mrs. Kawaii had an idea.

"What if we go to the border between Kawaii Altar and Lintercrest to see if the ring and scroll I left for Bri-Bri are still there...."

"That will work," said Mr. Kawaii.

Mr. Kawaii had to explain to Prince Kale about the ring and the scroll that they had left earlier. So they booked tickets on a first-class flight and flew to Lintercrest international airport. They rented a car and drove to the border.

The items Mrs. Kawaii put in the portal previously were no longer there.

"They're gone!" shouted Mrs. Kawaii.

"Both the ring and the scroll?" asked Mr. Kawaii.

"Yes, both," replied Mrs. Kawaii.

"Hmm...," Mr. Kawaii sank into his own thinking.

他們仍然沒有頭緒，他們沒辦法確定東西是被布理布理或是別人拿走的。他們開車前往可愛怡聖壇，途中在一個客棧停下來吃午飯。當他們正在吃三明治的時候，客棧的經理恰好經過他們用餐的桌子。經理看到那個 3D 列印出來的若薇亞公主洋娃娃正放在桌子上。

「藍頭髮的女孩！」那個經理倒吸了一口氣。

可愛怡太太抬頭看他，問說：

「什麼？你認識她嗎？」

「她和一群旅行者在這裡待過一個晚上，大概是三個星期前的事。」

卡爾王子很興奮地問：

「然後呢？你有沒有跟她或是他們當中的任何一個人說話？」

「並沒有……」那經理的臉突然變色，猶豫起來。

「你有沒有看到一個小男孩，大概八歲左右？他應該跟這個女孩是在一起的。」可愛怡先生很焦急地問。

「嗯……我還有事，要走了……」那個經理看起來似乎在隱藏著什麼，想要擺脫他們的盤問。

卡爾王子用力一把抓住他的手，說：

「等一等！一定有些什麼事！你一定要告訴我們！我們正在急切地尋找他們。這個女孩是我的妹妹，而那個小男孩是這對善良的夫婦失蹤已久的寶貝兒子。」

Still they had no clues. They could not even be sure that the things were taken by Bri-Bri or others. They drove into Kawaii Altar and stopped by an inn for lunch. While they were eating sandwiches, the manager of the inn walked by their table. The manager spotted the 3-D printed doll of Princess Rovia on the table.

"This blue-haired girl!" the manager gasped.

Mrs. Kawaii looked up and asked, "What? Do you know her?"

"She and a group of travelers stayed here for a night, about 3 weeks ago."

Prince Kale was so excited, he asked, "And? Did you get to talk to her? Or anyone of them?"

"Not really…," the manager's face suddenly changed and started to falter.

"Did you see a little boy who is about 8 years old? He should be with this girl," Mrs. Kawaii was anxious.

"Um… I need to go…," the manager looked like he was hiding something and trying to ditch the conversation.

Prince Kale grabbed his arm with force, "Wait! There was something. You have to tell us! We are earnestly looking for them. This girl is my sister and the little boy is this nice couple's missing son."

那個經理很關切地看著他們，然後嘆了一口氣：

「那個女孩，她意外死了，就在這個客棧裡。」

卡爾王子驚呆住。

「那個小男孩呢？」可愛怡太太的聲音顫抖著。

「他沒事，據我所知其他人都沒事......」經理回答。

可愛怡夫婦鬆了一口氣。

「她是怎麼死的？」卡爾王子緩慢地問著，眼裡充滿了淚水。

「我也不是很清楚......」經理回答，「我聽說她好像是從哪裡跌下來死的。」

「那發生事情之後他們做了什麼？去了哪裡？」可愛怡先生問。

「我不知道，很抱歉。」經理回答。「但是不知道為什麼，那個死掉的女孩變成了一個可以看得見的鬼魂。我想她還是跟著那一群人在一起。」

卡爾王子的眼睛亮了起來。

「他們離開得很匆忙。」經理繼續說，「他們看來好像在躲什麼人，非常害怕的樣子。」

The manager looked at them with concerns. Then he sighed, "The girl, she died in an accident, right here in this inn."

Prince Kale was dumbstruck.

"How about the little boy?" Mrs. Kawaii's voice was trembling when she asked.

"He was fine, so was everyone else in the group... as far as I know," said the manager.

Both Mr. and Mrs. Kawaii were relieved hearing it.

"How did she die?" Prince Kale asked slowly, his eyes were full of tears.

"I'm not sure exactly...," said the manager. "But I heard that she fell."

"Then what did they do after that? Do you know where they went?" asked Mr. Kawaii.

"I don't know, sorry...," replied the manager. "But for some reason that dead girl turned into a ghost, her spirit was visible. I think she was still with the group."

Prince Kale's eyes brightened up again.

"They left hastily," the manager continued. "They acted like someone was chasing them and they were terrified."

一個女服務生在叫喚經理，所以他就藉機離開了。

經過了一陣的沉默，可愛怡先生問說：

「所以，我們接下來要去哪裡？」

「我想我們可以試一個地方，雖然我只是用猜的。」
卡爾王子說。

「哪裡？」可愛怡夫婦異口同聲地問。

「我以前經常去一個叫做納威口的地方打獵。我妹妹
總是央求我帶她一起去，可是我從來沒有帶她去過。如果
她離開了波理斯瑪，可能會想要去那裡。如果她還跟那一
群人在一起的話，也許我們可以打聽到一些關於這些旅行
者的蛛絲馬跡。」

A waitresses was calling out to the manager, so he excused himself and left.

After a moment of silence among all of them, Mr. Kawaii asked, "So, where should we go next?"

"I think we can try a place, though it's simply a guess," said Prince Kale.

"Where?" Mr. and Mrs. Kawaii asked.

"I used to go to this place called Nawico to hunt. My sister always begged me to take her when I went hunting, but I never did. She would probably go there after she left Purisima. And if she is still with this group of people, maybe we can find some trace over there," said Prince Kale.

第二十四章 茅屋的不速之客

　　當可愛怡夫婦一抵達納威口，就被這裡的自然美景所震驚。卡爾王子告訴他們納威口是個天然野生的區域，這裡的人都住在森林裡的茅屋，以打獵爲生。他們將捕獲來的動物宰煮來吃，成爲食物。每一個聚落都與另一個聚落距離很遠，這樣他們才會有足夠大的領地去獵捕動物，好養活聚落裡的居民。可愛怡夫婦並不是很習慣這樣的生活方式，但是卡爾王子卻非常熟悉。

　　他們走進森林的深處，靠近因努區的邊界。當他們停下來休息的時候，可愛怡太太看見一個女孩，她以爲可能是若薇亞公主，便用眼神示意可愛怡先生和卡爾王子，讓他們知道。那個女孩子穿著白綠混紡的長衫，但是她的頭髮並不是藍色，而是黑色的。她正在採集各種不同的蔬菜及香草，放進籃子裡。

　　「嗨！」卡爾王子從遠處向她打招呼。

　　那女孩轉過身來，看著他們。她很訝異，也有一點緊張，但是她並沒有說什麼。

Chapter XXIV Unexpected Guests of the Hut

When Mr. and Mrs. Kawaii landed in Nawico, they were stunned by the beauty of all the nature. Prince Kale told them that Nawico was a wild place where people lived in the forest and hunted. They cooked animals they captured and killed for food. Each community of huts had to be far from the other, so the land each community hunted on was enough to feed all the people. Mr. and Mrs. Kawaii were not used to this type of living, but Prince Kale knew it pretty well.

They went deep in the forest, right on the border to Yinu. When they stopped for a break, Mrs. Kawaii spotted a girl whom she thought might be Princess Rovia. She alerted Mr. Kawaii and Prince Kale. It was a girl wearing a white and green gown, but her hair was not blue, it's black. The girl was collecting varieties of vegetables and herbs, putting them inside a basket.

"Hi," said Prince Kale from a distance.

The girl turned around and looked at them. She was surprised and a little nervous, but she did not say anything.

「我說，哈囉，妳好！」卡爾王子溫和地笑著，試著不要把她嚇跑。

那女孩撿起一個樹枝，在地上寫著：

「我不能說話。」

「哦！我很抱歉。」卡爾王子道歉說。「妳住在附近嗎？」

她點點頭。

「我們是訪客。我們到這裡來為了找我們失蹤的家人。」可愛怡太太很友善地說。

那女孩開始放鬆一些，因為覺得他們看起來的確不像壞人。他們三個人就向她走近。

「你知道這附近有什麼地方我們可以留下來過夜並用餐嗎?」可愛怡先生問。「這裡看起來不像可以找到旅館的樣子。」

"I said hello," said Prince Kale, smiling gently and trying not to scare her away.

The girl picked up a stick and wrote on the ground, "I can't talk."

"Oh, I am sorry," Prince Kale apologized. "Do you live nearby?"

The girl nodded her head.

"We are visitors. We are here because we are looking for some missing people from our family," Mrs. Kawaii talked friendly.

The girl started to relax a bit because they did not look like bad people. So the three of them walked towards her.

"Do you know any place we can stay for dinner and the night?" asked Mr. Kawaii. "It doesn't look like we can find an inn or hotel around here."

女孩搖搖頭，在地上寫：

「我可以問我叔叔，他也許會好心地願意讓你們過夜。」然後她指向一個方向，用她的雙手在空中比劃了一個三角形的形狀。

「那太棒了！」卡爾王子對她笑著說。

女孩也對他笑，彎腰去撿起地上的籃子。

「妳不介意的話，我可以來幫妳提籃子嗎？」卡爾王子說，就幫她把籃子提起來。

女孩有一點害羞，因為卡爾王子長得很帥，又強壯，還非常體貼。她用唇語說「謝謝」來表達謝意。

他們跟著她走，樹林越來越稀疏，可以開始看到天空。他們來到一個小村落，大約有十來戶茅草房。女孩領他們進入一個門前掛有風鈴和羽毛的茅屋。

卡爾王子和可愛怡夫婦隨著那女孩進去。他們看見一個男人坐在角落，正在給一個死掉的動物剝皮。在他身邊，坐著兩個少年人。女孩對他們用唇語說了些什麼，然後其中一個男孩說：

「她說這幾個訪客需要一個過夜的地方。」

那個高大的男人站起來，朗聲笑著，說：

「當然！歡迎到因努和納威口！你們想停留多久都沒問題，只要能夠習慣和我們一樣的生活方式！」

The girl shook her head, then wrote on the ground:

"I can ask my uncle. He may be kind enough to let you stay in his hut for the night." Then she pointed to a direction and drew a triangle in the air using her hands.

"That will be great!" said Prince Kale, smiling at her.

The girl smiled back and bent over to pick up her basket.

"Do you mind if I help you with the basket?" said Prince Kale as he lifted up the basket for her.

The girl was a little shy because Prince Kale was handsome, strong, and also very considerate. She expressed her appreciation by mouthing "thank you".

As they followed the girl, the trees began to grow skinnier, and they could soon see the sky. They came to a small village with a dozen of huts. The girl led them into a hut with a chime and a feather hung at the door.

Prince Kale, Mr. and Mrs. Kawaii walked in after the girl. They saw a big man sitting at the corner, he was skinning an animal. Next to him, sat two teen-aged boys. The girl mouthed something to the man, then one of the boys said,

"She says these visitors need a place to stay for the night."

The big man stood up and laughed brightly, "Of course! Welcome to Yinu and Nawico! You can stay as long as you like. Just eat and live like us!"

「謝謝你的大方招待！」可愛怡先生說。

然後卡爾王子前去幫忙那男人剝獸皮。

當那個女孩正在清洗撿來的植物，並把它們放入鍋中要煮湯時，另一個女孩從門簾後面走出來。這個女孩比較高，紅色的短髮，臉上有雀斑。她看起來比之前那個女孩大個幾歲。

可愛怡先生和太太兩個人一直盯著她看，然後大叫出來：

「可愛怡家族的拯救者！」

每個人都被這叫聲嚇了一跳，轉過來看他們。

「這個女孩……她長得跟照片上的一模一樣！就是給我們家族的那個預言。」可愛怡先生高聲說道，仍然不敢相信他自己的眼睛。

「哦！我的天啊！」可愛怡太太興奮地叫著。「是真的！預言就要發生了！」

那兩個少年人，一個有著怒髮衝冠的奇特髮型，另一個就是幫啞巴少女作翻譯的，他們兩人張大了眼睛，不是在看那個拯救者女孩，而是瞪著可愛怡夫婦在看。他們倆不約而同地叫出來：

「你們是布理布理的爸爸媽媽？！」

"Thank you! It's very generous of you!" said Mr. Kawaii.

Then Prince Kale went to help the man skinning the animal.

While the girl was washing and putting the plants into a pot to cook some soup, another girl walked in from behind a curtain. This girl was taller, with red short hair and freckles on her cheeks. She looked a few years older than the first girl.

Mr. and Mrs. Kawaii could not help gazing at her, then they cried out, "The savior of Kawaii!"

Everyone was shocked by this comment and turned around to look at them.

"This girl... she looks exactly the same as the one in the picture! A prophecy about our family," Mr. Kawaii exclaimed, still could not believe his own eyes.

"Oh my God!" Mrs. Kawaii was so excited. "It's true! And it's going to happen!"

Both the spiky-haired boy and the translation boy had their eyes wide open, not looking at that savior girl, but at the couple. They shouted at the exact same time,

"You are Bri-Bri's parents?!"

第二十五章　# 樂凡第的陌生人

　　真要昇這一組人藉著「靈魂之風」很迅速地來到並降落在樂凡第。真要昇又恢復了以前的快樂，因為他終於和他心愛的若薇亞公主重聚了。布理布理仍然急著要趕快去找他的家人。

　　「我要我的家人！」布理布理唉唉叫。

　　「當克喜回來之後，我們就可以用他的遠距傳送機器去尋找你的家人了。」蝦肉安慰他。

　　「我已經夠大了，知道什麼是蟲洞！」布理布理說。

　　當他們進入樂凡第裡面的浮島時，他們開始猜想，克喜他們是否已經到了，正在等他們。畢竟克喜他們的任務應該是比真要昇他們的還要簡單的。

　　「克喜他們有 41.8500620347%的機率會在這裡。但是如果他故意要和我們惡作劇、不讓我們找到的話，那機率就是 76.4%。」將安說。

Chapter XXV The Strange Man in La Frontier

TruEthan's group landed in La Frontier quickly. The Wind of the Soul was very efficient. TruEthan felt as happy as ever, finally reunited with his dearest Princess Rovia. Bri-Bri was still anxious about finding his family.

"I want my family!" whined Bri-Bri.

"When Chrishie joins us, we can use his little teleportation thingy to easily get to your family," said Sharo.

"I'm old enough to know what a wormhole is!" said Bri-Bri.

As the group entered the floating islands of La Frontier, they started to wonder if Chrishie was already there waiting for them. After all, Chrishie's task seemed so much easier than theirs.

"Chrishie has a 41.8500620347% chance of being here. But if he's pranking us, then the chance is 76.4%," said John.

「所以，你是說，他可能會在這裡，也可能不會在。」眞要昇說。

「是呀！」將安得意洋洋地回答。

眞要昇在想克喜是否能夠如期回到這裡。他的頭腦裡充斥著許多問題：

克喜他們現在安全嗎？我們當初決定分開是對的嗎？他們是否已找到紫羅蘭花的解藥？會不會強柯又跑去攻擊他們？他們會不會死在因努？不，不，不，我們會有相同的命運，如若薇亞在信中曾說的，會一起在大戰役中戰鬥——「血會濺出更多的血，和平非常遙遠」……

眞要昇的心裡閃過許多念頭，他無法把這些想法懸著，他必需找個人談談。

「蝦肉，對於那場戰役，你有任何線索什麼時候會發生嗎？」

「好問題。我覺得在我們還沒碰到克喜他們之前，應該是不會發生的。」

「我也是這麼想。」眞要昇嘆了一口氣。

眞要昇感覺到一陣焦慮的疼痛，但是身爲一個領導者，他決定在大家昏頭之前先找個地方休息，養精蓄銳。

"So, you basically mean he *might and might not* be here," said TruEthan.

"Yup!" John responded, smugly.

TruEthan started to imagine whether Chrishie would make it here in time. His brain was filled with different questions:

Are Chrishie and his group safe now? Was it right from the beginning to separate from him? Have they figured out the cure with violets? What if Jrunk hunted them down after we left? What if they die in Yinu? No, no, no, we share the same destiny to fight in the great battle that Rovia mentioned in her letter — "Blood will spill more blood, and the peace is far…."

TruEthan's mind raced with so many thoughts. He couldn't keep the suspense. He had to discuss it with someone.

"Sharo," said TruEthan, "Do you have any clues when the great battle will happen?"

"Good question," answered Sharo. "I'm guessing it won't happen until we meet up with Chrishie."

"That's what I thought, too," TruEthan sighed.

TruEthan felt a pang of worry. But as a leader, he decided that he had to rest and relax before getting everyone lost.

「晚上七點了，我們得找個地方過夜。」眞要昇說。

「在樂凡第南邊有好一些住宿的旅館，如果我們現在往那兒去，應該在八點之前可以到。」布理布理說。

「是啊，我想你們都需要好好休息。」若薇亞公主說，用她那虛無飄渺的眼神看著眞要昇。

當他們終於到了下榻的旅館時，已經晚上八點。若薇亞公主在外面的花園裡逛（身爲鬼魂的她一點也不累）。當他們在登記入住時，有另一個男人也在登記入住。當櫃台的服務人員正在準備房間的鑰匙時，那個男人盯著眞要昇這群人看。

「你們以前來過這裡嗎？」他問。

「是的，我們來過。」眞要昇回答，打量著那個男人。他是一個削瘦的中年男子，脖子上圍著一個黑色的絲巾。

「這樣啊……我沒有來過。」男人說得有一點陰鬱。

「如果你想要的話，我們可以帶你到處逛逛。」布理布理主動提議。

「謝謝。」男人淡淡地笑了一下。「我花了很遠的路程才來到這裡。到一個這樣熱鬧的地方有時會讓我覺得很寂寞，我已經忘了如何和人們談話、交朋友。」他的眼神很空洞。「還有，如何快樂。」

"It's about 7 p.m.," said TruEthan. "We should find somewhere to spend the night."

"There are some hotels in the southern part of La Frontier. If we go now, we could probably make it just before 8," said Bri-Bri.

"Yes, I think you people need your rest," said Princess Rovia, casting a glance at TruEthan with care in her ghostly and mysterious eyes.

When they finally got to the hotel, it was already past 8 p.m. Princess Rovia was outside in the garden (she was not tired at all being a ghost). While they were checking in, a man walked in to check into the hotel as well. While the receptionist was getting the keys ready, the man was looking at TruEthan and his group.

"Have you come here before?" asked the man.

"Yes, we have," answered TruEthan, looking at him. He was a skinny middle-aged man, wearing a black scarf on his neck.

"I see. I haven't," said the man gloomily.

"We could show you around if you want," Bri-Bri offered.

"Thank you," the man smiled faintly. "I came a long way to be here. It sometimes makes me feel lonely when I come to a place full of people. I have forgotten what it's like to be social," his eyes were blank, "...and to be happy."

「我替你感到難過。」眞要昇說。

不知爲什麼，蝦肉覺得有某種熟悉的感覺，一種要命的似曾相識的感覺，卻想不起來是什麼。

"I feel sorry for you," said Bri-Bri.

Somehow Sharo felt something seemed familiar, awfully familiar.

第二十六章　樂凡第一日遊

　　隔天早上，眞要昇他們和那個男人在用早餐時碰到。

　　「今天你會想要跟我們一起出去玩玩嗎？」眞要昇問他。

　　「我知道幾個好玩的景點！」布理布理很興奮地說。

　　「我很樂意。」那個男人笑著說。

　　布理布理列出一些有名的博物館、展場、店鋪、景點、山區等。

　　「我贊成先去翠尼提展場！」布理布理說。他喜歡有熱鬧人群及商店的地方。

　　「我想去『王室博物館』。」那個男人說。「我一直想知道在佛夢達裡面不同跳越區的國王與女王的歷史。」

　　「好主意！」蝦肉附和。「我們在那裡可以學到一些歷史。」他很喜歡去逛博物館。

　　「這樣就夠我們玩一整天了！」眞要昇說。

Chapter XXVI The Tour in La Frontier

In the morning, TruEthan's group met up with the man for breakfast.

"Do you want to join us doing something fun today?" asked TruEthan to the man.

"I know some fun spots we could go to!" said Bri-Bri, excitedly.

"I'll be pleased to," said the man, smiling.

Bri-Bri made a list of the most famous museums, fairs, shops, vista points, and mountains.

"I vote we should go to Trinity fair!" said Bri-Bri. He likes places with crowds and shops.

"I actually want to go to the Kings and Queens Museum", said the man. "I've always wanted to learn about the kings and queens of different Jumpers in Formonda."

"Good thinking!" said Sharo. "We could all learn a bit of history there!" Sharo loved going to museums.

"Well, that will wrap up the day," said TruEthan.

「我們走吧！」布理布理說。

他們先出發到翠尼提展場。翠尼提這名字本來是來自翠尼提島，就是後來的「可愛怡之島」（布理布理的家人以前住的地方）。有另一個島叫做文西洛色提島，在古老的樂凡第語言裡，意思是「不停止的勇者」。這兩個浮島在樂凡第都很有名。

這個展覽是在夏天的時候舉行，從七月 26 號開始，維持一個月，爲了紀念樂凡第把翠尼提島從「阿努比斯之臉」的領土中奪過來。在這個展覽裡，有雲霄飛車，摩天輪，還有許多可以贏得獎品的遊戲區。

當眞要昇他們和那個男人去坐雲霄飛車時，布理布理把他的手舉到空中，大喊著：「太棒了！」除了那個男人之外，每個人都跟著這麼做。當他們下來之後，那個男人就吐了。

然後他們決定去玩遊戲。

「我想要贏一個絨毛老鼠娃娃！」布理布理說，準備著要投擲圈圈。他連續投進了三個，都落在很遠的同一根桿子裡。

「恭喜啊！」遊戲站的管理員說，「你得到一個超級大的絨毛老鼠娃娃！」

「YAY！」布理布理高興雀躍。

"Let's get going then!" said Bri-Bri.

They set off first to Trinity fair, named after Trinity Island, now known as the Island of Kawaii (where Bri-Bri's family used to live). There was another floating island called Vencilocity Island, which means "the brave that never stops" in the ancient Frontier language. These two floating islands in La Frontier were both famous.

This fair took place in the summer, starting on July 26th and continuing for a month, in honor of La Frontier winning Trinity Island over from the Face of Anubis. In the Trinity fair, there were roller coasters, Ferris wheels, and booths with prizes that you could win. When TruEthan's group and the strange man went on the roller coaster, Bri-Bri put his hands in the air and yelled "this is awesome". Everyone else did the same, except the strange man. When they got off, he threw up.

They decided to go play the games at the booths instead.

"I want to win a little mousey stuff animal!" said Bri-Bri, ready for ring-toss. He tosses 3 rings in a row, they all landed on the same stick on the far end.

"Congratulations!" said the person who ran the booth. "You got yourself a big, big, big stuffed mousey!"

"Yay!" Bri-Bri was jubilant.

「我也想試試看。」那個陌生男人說。

他投擲了三個圈，只有一個投進到最靠近他自己的那根桿子裡。

「喔，抱歉，」遊戲站管理員說，「你只能得到一個小的絨毛蜥蜴娃娃。」

「沒關係。」那個男人說，收下了那個娃娃。

「我們接下來可以去王室博物館了。」眞要昇說。

他們走了約二十分鐘，來到博物館。當他們進去後，那個男人臉上充滿了好奇的表情。

「看！那是馮艾夫莉女王的畫像，樂凡第的第一個皇后！哇！看哪，這是馮艾夫芭絲女王嬰孩的時候！那個是倒楣九世女王！」蝦肉以前來過這裡，所以他如數家珍。

「看！這是她的女兒愛斯基諾公主，她嫁給伯瑞王子，生了希非念和羅斯提。」

每個人多多少少學到了一些關於樂凡第的歷史。然後他們繼續往前走，到了波理斯瑪那一區。若薇亞公主知道這裡的每一個皇室成員。

「看！拉瑪皇后和她的妹妹拉杜。還有，拉基國王，拉費國王，拉皮國王！」

"I wanna try, too," said the strange man.

He tossed all three rings, only one of them made it on the stick nearest to him.

"Awww, sorry," said the man who ran the booth. "You get a little stuffed lizard."

"Okay," said the man, taking the lizard.

"We can go to the Kings and Queens Museum next," said TruEthan.

It took them about 20 minutes to walk to the museum. When they went in, the strange man had a curious look on his face.

"Look! That's a portrait of Queen VanEvery, the first queen of La Frontier. Aww, look! That's baby Queen VonEvirbath! There's Queen Doom IX!" Sharo had been here before, so he knew a lot.

"Look! It's her daughter Princess Eskino, who married Prince Blurei and had their children Silverneim and Rosettte!"

Everybody now knew something about La Frontier. Then they moved on to the Purisima section. Princess Rovia knew every single one of them.

"Look! That's Queen La Mar with her sister La Tu! More here…. King La Ki, La Fi, and La Pi!"

每個人都在笑。

「是啦！我知道以前他們的名字都……又簡單又好記。後來就演化得越來越複雜了，像是沙序提二十七世女王，阿樓丟沃費亞國王，還有立弗其瑙立思提諾女王。」

布理布理用手掌拍自己的額頭。

「啊！那個是倒楣九世女王在還沒來到樂凡第、嫁給力諾馮黑里歐國王之前的樣子。最後，這是馮史曼國王和莎夏皇后，他們就是我和卡爾王子的祖父母！」

他們繼續走，布理布理認出了可愛怡聖壇早期的皇室成員。

「那是滿治先生！」布理布理說。「我很確定那是滿治先生和他的太太佩子。我想這個人應該是滿治先生的兒子，棕左天皇。」

他繼續說，「那是滿治先生的孫子，仁至天皇。喔！我的天啊！那個是有名的西維和加古素，還有他們的兒子可禮。可禮和威敏生了可愛怡，從此開始了可愛怡家族。」

當他們逛完博物館的時候，每個人的頭腦裡都被這些名字充斥得快要爆炸了。他們決定告一段落，打道回府去休息。

Everyone chuckled.

"Ya, I know. Their names in the very early days were... simple, but easy to remember. They evolved to become more and more complicated later. For example, that's Queen Sachitit XXVII, King Alodio O'Via, and Queen Lifokinoalistino."

Bri-Bri face-palmed himself.

"Ah! That's Queen Doom IX before she married to the King Lino VonHeliot in La Frontier. Then, lastly, King VonSman and Queen Sasha, the grandparents of me and my brother Prince Kale!"

As they moved on, Bri-Bri started to recognize the kings and queens of Kawaii Altar from the early days.

"That's Majino!" said Bri-Bri, "I'm pretty sure that's Majino and his wife, Pinuku. And I think that guy is Majino's son, Emperor Sawudo."

He continued. "That's Majino's grandson, Emperor Renji. Oh my god! That's the famous Sylvia and Jagarosu, and their son Klim! Klim and Welming had Kawaii who went off and started the Kawaii family! "

When they were done with the museum, their heads were exploding with all these names and knowledge. They decided to call it off for the day and head back to the hotel.

在回去旅館的路上，那個男人發現了一家店，叫做「金珍飲」。他就跟其他人告辭，自己一個人走進去。過了幾個小時，其他人都在旅館休息夠了，他們就過來找他。他們走進店裡，看見那個男人正在大口大口地狂飲一瓶又一瓶的酒。他看起來很自在，好像完全忘卻了煩惱。他說著一些莫名其妙的話，像是「把我的烏龜還給我」，「家家卡特力師啊咧」這種沒有意義的字眼。

真要昇有點擔心他，便走到他身邊，問他說：

「你喝醉了嗎？」

On their way back to the hotel, the strange man noticed a shop. The shop was called "Precious Golden Liquid". He excused himself from the group and walked in. After a couple of hours of resting in the hotel, TruEthan's group went back to find him. They walked into the shop and found the strange man gulping down bottles and bottles of wine. He looked very relaxed and carefree though. He was saying something random or meaningless like "Give me my turtles", "Jajacatarisu Ali", etc. Nobody could understand what he was saying.

TruEthan was a bit concerned. So he came to the side of the man and asked,

"You're drunk?"

第二十七章 # 黑暗與光明

「是啊！我是強柯勒萬。」那個男人說。

「什麼？」布理布理和眞要昇異口同聲，似乎沒有聽清楚他講的是什麼。

「我的老天！你是強柯！」蝦肉尖叫。

「是啊！你們剛才不是就問我了嗎？」男人含糊不清地說。

「不！我們是問說你是不是喝醉了！」將安說。（註：英文的「喝醉」drunk 和「強柯」的名字 Jrunk 發音相同。）

「對，喝醉的那個字，D 開頭的。」眞要昇說。

「喔！那個字……也是啦！我也是喝醉了啊！但是，我，還是，強柯── 勒萬。」

男人拿下喬裝，露出他的眞面目。每一個人，包括店長和顧客，都睜大眼睛瞪著強柯，一片安靜無聲。

「去死吧！」強柯在一片死寂中突然咆哮起來。

Chapter XXVII The Darkness and the Light

"Yes, I am Jrunk Lerwan," said the strange man.

"What?" Bri-Bri and TruEthan were not quite sure about what they heard.

"Oh My God! You're Jrunk!" Sharo screamed.

"Yes, wasn't that what you said in the first place?" the man was mumbling.

"No! We just thought you were drunk from drinking," said John.

"Right, drunk with a D," said TruEthan.

"Oh, that drunk! Well, yes, I am that drunk, too. But, still, I — am — Jrunk — Lerwan."

The man took off the disguise and showed his true face. Everyone, including the store manager and all the customers, stared at Jrunk with wide eyes and stunned silence.

"Die!" Jrunk suddenly howled after a few moments of silence.

　　黑暗開始在他身邊出現，形成一團一團泡泡狀且搖晃延伸的手臂。強柯使出來的這種泡泡裡面充滿了邪惡，會自動去攻擊傷害人，還會發射出許多黑暗的碎片，就是當時害死了若薇亞公主的那種。

　　蝦肉在嘗試躲避這些黑暗碎片時，不禁開始想起若薇亞公主是怎麼死的。

　　到底是什麼讓她有能力可以幫助布理布理找到家人？他問他自己。她被殺死的時候我好像看到什麼東西，是跟布理布理的家人有關的……

　　蝦肉撇了布理布理一眼，當初大家在一起的任務就是為了幫布理布理找他的父母，不是嗎？然後他把眼光移開，到若薇亞公主身上，她的靈體正飄浮在空中。接著他回想起在可愛怡聖壇那天晚上發生的細節。就在此時，蝦肉感到他的小腿周圍一陣緊繃。他低頭一看，驚恐地發現有黑暗的碎片正在包圍他的腳。

　　不！我不能死！我一定要解開迷團！

　　他很快地抓起那些黑暗碎片，用盡吃奶的力氣，丟向強柯。現在他想起來了，在林特魁司那裡拿到的戒指！當他們在客棧被強柯攻擊的那天晚上，有一個黑暗碎片帶走了布理布理手上的戒指，然後去了若薇亞公主的房間。

Darkness started to appear around his body and form little bobbly wobbly arms. Jrunk's darkness is a blob filled with evil which makes it attack people. It fired little pieces of darkness, the same ones that killed Princess Rovia before.

Sharo started to think about how Princess Rovia died, while trying to dodge the pieces of darkness.

What made me think that she was going to help Bri-Bri find his family? He asked himself. *I believe I saw something related to Bri-Bri's family when she was killed….*

Sharo cast a glance at Bri-Bri — they first started the mission because of him, right? He then moved his gaze to Princess Rovia, her spirit was hanging in the air. Then he continued to recall what happened when they stayed for the night at Kawaii Altar. Right at this moment, Sharo felt a tight grip around his legs. He looked down and was horrified finding that there were pieces of darkness wrapping around his feet.

No! I cannot die before I solve the mystery!

He instantly grabbed those pieces of darkness, with all his might, and flung them back at Jrunk. Now he remembered everything — the ring from Lintercrest! At the night when they first got attacked by Jrunk's darkness, a piece of darkness slid up Bri-Bri and grabbed the ring, it then went to Princess Rovia's room.

　　一定是在她死的時候滑到了她的手上！這就是為什麼她可以引導布理布理找到家人。這樣我就瞭了！

　　就在這時候，若薇亞公主正被黑暗包圍起來，強柯打算再次把她擄走。真要昇皺起眉頭，大喊：

　　「放開她！」

　　他從身邊的餐桌上抓起一個牛排刀，擲向那團黑暗泡泡。刀子劃過黑暗泡泡，造成一個小小的洞，但是很快就又自己癒合了。

　　不知從哪兒來的一陣強光突然照亮了整個地方。那白光強烈到讓每個人的眼睛都暫時看不見了，包括強柯。那光似乎把那些黑暗碎片都包圍起來，讓它們立時消失不見。強柯知道自己贏不過，就立時逃逸。當黑暗都不見了，光也漸漸退去。

　　正當大家的眼睛都還在適應時，蝦肉瞥見到阿米，手上拿著一個超級手電筒，而克喜正在跑向真要昇。

The ring must have slid on her when she died, and that's why her destiny is to find Bri-Bri's parents! Now it makes more sense!

At the same time Princess Rovia was surrounded by darkness. It was trying to wrap her up and abduct her again. TruEthan scowled and cried out, "Let go of her!" He grabbed a knife from the table near him and threw it to that darkness blob. It cut through the darkness with a tiny hole but the darkness sealed up by itself again.

Out of nowhere, a super bright light suddenly lit up the whole place. The light was so white and bright that it blinded everyone, including Jrunk. The darkness started to shrink, and soon you couldn't see it against the blazing white light. The light seemed to wrap around the darkness as it disappeared. Knowing he could not win, Jrunk made himself disappear in an instant. When the darkness was no longer visible, the light was fading, too.

While people were still adjusting their eyes, Sharo caught a glimpse of Armi holding his super flashlight and Chrishie running towards TruEthan.

「真要昇！」克喜快樂地大叫。

「克喜！」真要昇也歡喜喊著。

他們跑向對方，擁抱在一起。

「你怎麼找到我們的？」真要昇興奮地問。

「我們不久前才來到樂凡第。其他人都要去休息，我和阿米就先出來，看看能不能打聽到你們的消息。當我們經過這附近時，看到有黑暗從窗戶和門縫中溢出來。阿米拿出他的超級手電筒來察看，我跟著他進來，就看到了你們。」

「我好高興你回來了！而且你還幫我們擊退了強柯！」真要昇說。

「現在我們知道阿米的超級手電筒可以保護我們不受強柯的黑暗攻擊了！」蝦肉說。

「其他人在哪裡呢？」將安問。

「他們正在旅館裡休息，大概兩英哩遠。」阿米回答。

"TruEthan!" yelled Chrishie with happiness.

"Chrishie!" yelled TruEthan with joy.

They ran towards each other and hugged.

"How did you find us?" asked TruEthan, excitedly.

"We just arrived at La Frontier not long ago. While the others were resting, Armi and I went to see if we could get some information about your group. When we passed this area, we saw darkness spilling out of the door and windows. Armi took out his super flashlight to investigate, and I followed him in. Then we found you guys."

"I'm so glad you're back, and you helped us defeat Jrunk!" said TruEthan.

"Now we know that Armi's super flashlight can protect us from Jrunk's darkness!" said Sharo.

"Where are the others?" asked John.

"They are staying in a hotel, about two miles away," replied Armi.

第二十八章 　大團聚

　　在回旅館的路上，穿過美麗的樂凡第市區，每個人卻因為剛才與強柯的那一仗累得說不出話，大家都筋疲力竭。只有布理布理是精神最好的，一直催著大家走快一點，因為他已經從克喜那邊聽到他的爸爸媽媽也跟著他們來到這裡了。其他人都走得很慢，好像剛剛才跑完了十公里的馬拉松一樣。若薇亞公主在前頭帶路，因為其他人都太累了，還有，因為布理布理的方向感很爛。

　　當他們跟著克喜和阿米來到他們的房間時，他們看到艾迪亞自己一個人坐在角落，潔兒和迷蝶互相靠著。可愛怡先生和太太正在交談：

　　「他們答應我們，會帶我們找到布理布理的……」可愛怡太太說到一半突然停住。

　　一個小孩衝過房間。

　　「媽媽！爸爸！」布理布理跑得像光速一樣快。

　　「布理布理！喔！真的是你？你長得這麼高了！」可愛怡太太把布理布理抱在懷裡，柔聲地說：「我好想你，我親愛的寶貝……」

Chapter XXVIII The Reunion

As they made their way back to the hotel through the beautiful city in La Frontier, everybody seemed quiet after the unexpected battle with Jrunk. They were all exhausted. Bri-Bri was the only one that was still energetic and urging the group to move faster because he had heard from Chrishie that his parents were here with the group. All others were slow, like they had run a 10K marathon. Princess Rovia was leading the way because everyone else was too tired, plus Bri-Bri's sense of direction sucked.

As they trudged in and reached Chrishie and Armi's room, they saw Adiale sitting in a corner trying to be alone, Jade and Misty leaning on each other. Then there were Mr. and Mrs. Kawaii talking.

"They promised us they would find Bri-Bri and…," Mrs. Kawaii suddenly stopped.

A child ran in the room. "Mommy! Daddy!" Bri-Bri ran forward at the speed of light.

"Bri-Bri! Oh! Is that you? You've grown so tall!" Mrs. Kawaii held Bri-Bri- in her arms and cooed, "I missed you so much, my dearest baby…."

「我也好想妳！在阿努比斯那裡的第一年，我每天晚上都哭著一個人上床睡覺。」布理布理啜泣著。

一開始大家以為他是傷心得哭了，後來才發現布理布理的笑容。眼淚從可愛怡夫婦的臉上流下，越來越多，像溪水一樣不停止。他們緊緊地互相擁抱，用盡最大的力氣。艾迪亞趕緊拿著潔兒和迷蝶的叔叔給她們的花盆，試圖接住他們歡喜的眼淚。

這時候，卡爾王子轉向若薇亞公主。她正飄浮在空中，看著卡爾王子。卡爾王子走向她，伸出手去。

「若薇亞！雖然妳現在是個鬼魂，那並不打緊。」卡爾王子說。「重要的是我終於還能再見到妳，雖然我不能擁抱妳。」

若薇亞公主笑著，她感覺好像有歡喜的眼淚要出來，但她是個鬼魂，流不出眼淚。

「當妳在到處歷險的這些時候，我一直都以為妳已經在波理斯瑪的那場大火中喪生了！沒想到我現在還能再見到妳。」卡爾王子伸出一隻手，想要摸摸他妹妹的臉頰，但是手卻穿了過去。

"I missed you so much, too! In the first year with Anubis, I cried every night when I went to bed alone," Bri-Bri started sobbing.

At first everyone thought he was crying for sadness, until they realized Bri-Bri actually was smiling. Tears dropped down from Mr. and Mrs. Kawaii's faces and grew to become streams that could not be stopped. They hugged each other so tight that it almost squeezed the living daylights out of each other. Adiale grabbed the flower pot that Jade and Misty's uncle gave them and tried to catch their tears of joy.

At this moment, Prince Kale turned to Princess Rovia, while Princess Rovia was floating in the air and looking at Prince Kale. Prince Kale went forward and reached an arm toward Princess Rovia.

"Rovia! It doesn't matter that you're a ghost," said Prince Kale. "It matters that I see you again, even though I can't hug you."

Princess Rovia smiled and felt like crying with tears of joy, but she was not able to cry any tears as a ghost.

"Of all the time when you went exploring and traveling, I thought you were dead in the wiped-out Jumper of Purisima. But I finally see you again." Prince Kale's reached his hand trying to touch his sister's cheek, but it simply went through.

「我們兩人各自有艱險漫長的旅程。」若薇亞公主說。「你已經在你的旅程中經歷了很多，而我，這些經驗都是全新的——各種的探索和冒險。然而，在這旅程中所遭遇的，不管是海洋、湖泊、森林、建築、村落、英雄，還是戰鬥，最棒的還是終於又能看到你！」

一滴眼淚從卡爾王子的臉上滑落，掉在艾迪亞捧著的花盆裡。

很神奇地，紫羅蘭的花朵開始綻放，一朵接一朵，總共開了七朵。艾迪亞摘下一朵，放進口中吃下去。

每個人都在注視，空氣中充滿了愛與希望。一切是那麼的安靜祥和，直到……

「唉！耳根清淨的時間結束了！」將安嘆氣說。大家轉頭看他。

「你就不能把你那討人厭的意見忍耐幾分鐘不要說嗎？」一個高頻率的聲音劃過空中。艾迪亞尖聲說著，臉上卻帶著一個奇怪的笑容。

他們有個歡樂的夜晚，談笑、擁抱，又唱又跳。

"I know that both our journeys have been long and hard," said Princess Rovia. "You've encountered a lot in your journeys as always. For me, this experience is new — exploring and adventure. However, as far as oceans, rivers, lakes, forests, structures, villains, heroes, and battles that I've encountered in this journey, meeting you again after so long is the best."

One teardrop came down Prince Kale's face and dropped into the flower pot that Adiale was holding.

Miraculously, flowers of violet grew and bloomed one after one. There were 7 in total. Adiale carefully picked one and ate it. Everyone watched, with the feeling of love and hope in the air. All was silent, until….

"Alas! The time of silence is over," sighed John, suddenly. Everyone turned to look at him.

"You just cannot keep your annoying comment quiet for a moment, can you?" The high-pitched voice of Adiale pierced through the air, along with a strange smile on her face.

They had a very fun night — laughing, talking, hugging, and dancing.

第二十九章 血的預兆

終於大家要休息了，準備就寢。「晚安」聲此起彼落，很快地每個人都陷入夢鄉之中。

睡夢中，眞要昇夢到「血會濺出更多的血」——這是當時若薇亞公主在信上告訴他的。他夢到一個在佛夢達前所未有的戰役，巨大又可怕。滿地是血，樹木也凋殘而死。河是紅色的，山崩地裂。天空是橘紅色的，反映著吞噬這些跳越區的死亡的顏色。最後，波理斯瑪在他的夢中出現，那個在現實中已經被大火摧毀的跳越區，那裡有一群旅行者，是他不認識的。他們在尋找某個具有重大意義的東西。然後，黑暗、血、骷髏頭，還有其他很多不祥的東西都一一出現。

眞要昇醒過來，心跳得很快，背上流了好多汗。

「媽呀！眞是一個嚇人的夢！」他心裡想。「看來像是一個超級大的戰爭，馬上要來了。這場戰爭中有誰呢？」

Chapter XXIX A Sign of Blood

Finally everyone got ready to rest and settle down. There was a chorus of "good nights". They all eventually fell into a deep sleep.

During the night, TruEthan had dreams about "blood will spill more blood", a line from Princess Rovia's letter before. He dreamed of the biggest battle ever in Formonda, so big and terrible. The land was covered in blood. The trees withered away and died. The rivers ran red. The mountains fell apart and became a big pile of rocks. The sky turned to orange and red, reflecting the color of death that swallowed the Jumpers. At the end, there was Purisima, the Jumper that had already been destroyed by fire in reality. There was a group of travelers, ones that he didn't recognize, that were searching for something. The quest had a meaning. Then, darkness, blood, skulls, and other bad things started to appear.

TruEthan woke up, his heart racing and a lot of sweat in his back.

"God! That was an intense dream!" he thought. "It seemed like the greatest battle, it's near. Who are in the battle?"

　　因爲惡夢的驚恐，眞要昇躺了好一會睡不著。後來他終於又睡著了，這一次還好沒有再作夢。

　　當克喜早上醒來的時候，房間裡其他每個人都已經醒來在聊天了。他們走到樓下去吃早餐。當他們坐下來時，眞要昇問克喜，是否可以單獨跟他說個話。

　　「當然！」克喜回答地很隨性。

　　結果要談的事完全不是克喜會想到的。他以爲眞要昇只是要聊聊朋友間的家常話題，或重聚後的溫馨與歡迎，但並不是。眞要昇一開始就說到血會覆蓋好幾個跳越區，植物凋萎，等等，還有死亡。克喜打了一個冷顫。

　　「有事要發生了！我們必須帶領這一群人度過佛夢達史上很可怕的一段時期。這會是一場大戰役，但是沒有人會來打這場仗，那些本地居民根本沒有能力來爲他們自己的生存奮戰。」眞要昇說。

　　「唉，當初我造佛夢達的時候，是要讓它成爲一個和平的地方，我不知道強柯這樣的壞人是怎麼跑出來的。」克喜說。

　　眞要昇嘆口氣說，「這不是重點，克喜。重點是，**我們**必須要戰鬥！**我們**必須要打這場仗，佛夢達才能安全！我們不能眼睜睜地讓佛夢達裡面的人被殺死。」

TruEthan could not sleep for a while because of the terror from the nightmare. When he finally fell asleep again, thankfully, there was no more dreaming this time.

When Chrishie woke up in the morning, everyone else in his room was already awake and chatting. They walked downstairs for breakfast. When they sat down with their breakfast, TruEthan asked Chrishie if they could talk in private.

"Sure!" Chrishie answered casually.

It wasn't what Chrishie had been expecting. He thought this was just a friendly chat about a little reunion and a warm welcome, but it wasn't. TruEthan started talking about blood covering the Jumpers and plants withering away... and death. Chrishie shuddered.

"Something is coming! We have to lead this group through a fearful time of Formonda history— this will be the Great Battle! Nobody will do it though, no locals or residents will be able to fight for their own lives," TruEthan said.

"Well, I created Formonda to be a peaceful place. I don't know how a person like Jrunk appeared," said Chrishie.

TruEthan sighed, "It's not about that, Chrishie. It's that WE have to fight! We have to fight so Formonda will be safe. We don't want people in Formonda to die!"

　　克喜盯著眞要昇幾秒鐘，然後說，「我們必須開始爲戰爭預備！現在就去警告大家！你說的一點也沒錯，除了我們六個人——你，我，阿米，艾迪亞、蝦肉、和將安，沒有人能做得到。我們必須爲佛夢達負責！」

　　眞要昇笑了，「這才是我的好朋友克喜。」

Chrishie stared at TruEthan for a few seconds, then he said, "We have to prepare for the battle! Go warn the others. You are absolutely right, no one except us, six of us — you, I, Armi, Adiale, Shao, and John, can do this. We are responsible for Formonda!"

TruEthan smiled, "Now that's my good friend Chrishie."

第三十章 # 惡人的協議

　　強柯來回踱步著，他想要找阿努比斯。

　　雖然強柯控制著巨大的黑暗，足以一次殺死一萬人，但要來一個空前絕後的戰役，他仍然需要一個搭檔和幫手。他猜阿努比斯在搶了可愛怡夫婦的錢之後，應該已經跑到某個被遺棄的地方躲起來。除了強柯的地盤勁剋司之外，另外兩個被遺棄的地方就是林特魁司和波理斯瑪。強柯決定先去波理斯瑪找找看。

　　強柯用他的黑暗魔法把他自己遠距傳送到波理斯瑪。當他到了那裡，除了廢墟和塵土之外，什麼也沒有。被大火吞噬燒盡之後，現在這裡是一片平坦。他很容易就可以看到阿努比斯，正在數著一張一張的鈔票。

　　強柯嚥了一口口水。他和阿努比斯都不是善於交際的人，這會有一點不太自然。

　　「嗯……你好。」強柯來到阿努比斯背後說。「我的名字是強柯，我想你應該聽說過我。」

　　阿努比斯轉過頭，瞇著眼瞧他。「你來找我幹嘛？」

Chapter XXX The Villains' Deal

Jrunk was pacing back and forth. He wanted to find Anubis.

Even though Jrunk controlled a great darkness that could kill 10,000 people, he still needed a partner and a backup for an unprecedented fight. He guessed that Anubis must have run to some deserted place after he robbed Mr. and Mrs. Kawaii. Other than Zinx, which was Jrunk's territory and base, there were only two deserted places, Lintercrest and Purisima. Jrunk decided to try looking in Purisima first.

Jrunk used his dark magic to teleport himself to Purisima. When he got there, there was nothing but debris and dirt. Burned down by the great fire, it was all flat now. It was pretty easy to spot Anubis there, counting the money, dollar by dollar.

Jrunk gulped. Neither he nor Anubis was really the social type. This would be awkward.

"Um… hello," said Jrunk when he came behind Anubis. "My name is Jrunk. I believe you have heard of me before."

Anubis turned around, squinting. "Why have you come to find me?"

「我需要你的幫忙。」強柯回答。「我正在計畫一場終極之戰。」

「嗯哼……」阿努比斯說，「你的目標是誰？」

「可愛怡。」強柯說，「整個可愛怡宗族。」

「啊！」阿努比斯從地上跳起來。「那將會是一場大戰！可愛怡宗族是整個佛夢達歷史上最有錢也最悠久的家族。」現在阿努比斯開始興致勃勃了。

「你打算要付我多少錢？」阿努比斯問。

「我沒有錢。」強柯說。

「喔！真可惜……」阿努比斯又坐回剛才的位置去。

「等等！我有一棟豪宅，在森林裡。還有一整個跳越區可以給你。那裡有很多資源，比如說核電廠。」強柯說，希望能打動阿努比斯。

「嗯，那些可以賣多少錢？」

「我猜好幾百萬，可能有上千萬。」

「是哪一個跳越區？」

「勁剋司。」強柯盡量不去想他因此會失去自己的家，雖然老實說他還更喜歡待在那種有酒吧的旅館裡。

"I need your help," replied Jrunk. "I'm planning for a terminating fight."

"Um hum," said Anubis. "Who is your target?"

"Kawaii," said Jrunk. "The entire Kawaii clan."

"Ooh!" Anubis jumped out of the ground. "That will be a BIG one! The Kawaii clan is the richest and longest family in the history of Formonda." Now Anubis showed a lot more interest.

"How much are you going to pay me?" Anubis asked.

"I don't have money," said Jrunk.

"Oh, too bad…," said Anubis, sitting back in his spot.

"Wait — I have a mansion in the woods and a whole Jumper that I can offer you. There are lots of resources, like nuclear energy," said Jrunk, hoping to convince Anubis.

"Well, how much can you sell it for?"

"I'm guessing a couple of millions, might even be a billion."

"Which Jumper is this?"

"Zinx," said Jrunk. He tried not to think about losing his home, even though he did like to stay at inns or hotels with bars more than his own home.

「那可愛怡家族的財寶呢？」阿努比斯問。天曉得他已經覬覦這個有多久了！

「全是你的。」強柯說。「我一毛錢也不要。」

「成交！」阿努比斯愉快地說著。「我們開始計畫吧！」

當他們在討論攻擊策略時，強柯才發現阿努比斯很善於狡猾的巧計。他們倆真是最佳拍檔。

「根據我的水晶魔球，」阿努比斯說，「克喜他們那幫人現在正在樂凡第的郊外。」

「太棒了！」

"How about the treasures and money of the Kawaii family?" asked Anubis. God knows how long he has been coveting it!

"They are all yours," replied Jrunk. "I won't take a penny."

"Deal!" Anubis said delightedly. "Let's plan!"

As they discussed the attacking strategies, Jrunk realized that Anubis was very good at scheming. It was a perfect match.

"According to my magic ball," said Anubis, "Chrishie and his gang are out in the field of La Frontier."

"Fantastic!"

第三十一章 上路了

在可愛怡聖壇這是很平常的一天。小小孩在公園裡玩耍，大小孩在學校裡上課，青少年在忙著通簡訊，大人們在工作。可愛怡聖壇一直以來都是可愛怡家族的領土，但是在這個有錢的可愛怡家族三年前遷徙過來之前，它並沒有被好好地發展。現在它是個朝氣蓬勃且非常現代化的城市，到處都是高樓大廈和高架橋，很多大型廣告看板懸掛在半空中。

在市中心廣場，有一群工作人員正在用起重機架設一個超大的表演帳棚，那是一個紅橘相間的帳棚，裡面足夠容納三萬人。

一個男人走過來，開始張貼海報：

林特魁司馬戲團

來看驚人的表演！

老虎、大象、馬、猴子、蛇，還有更多！

我們還有跳火圈和空中飛人！

完全免費！

地點：可愛怡聖壇，市中心廣場

Chapter XXXI On the Way

It was a typical day in Kawaii Altar. Small kids were playing in the parks, bigger kids were studying in the school, teenagers were texting, and adults were working. Kawaii Altar had been the territory of Kawaii for a long time, but not very well developed until the entire clan of rich Kawaii family migrated here 3 years ago. Now it was a vibrant and modern city, full of skyscrapers and overpasses, with big advertising signs hung in the sky.

At the central square of the city, a crew was setting up a huge tent using tower cranes. It was a big orange and red tent that had enough room inside to fit 30,000 people.

A man came along and started putting up posters.

LINTERCREST CIRCUS
COME SEE THE AMAZING SHOW WITH TIGERS,
ELEPHANTS, HORSES, MONKEYS, SNAKES, AND
MORE!!
WE ALSO HAVE HOOPS OF FIRE AND ACROBATS!!
PLUS... IT IS FREE!!!
Location: City Square of Kawaii Altar
Time: This Saturday 1:20 p.m.

人們好奇地湧過來張望海報的內容。

「哇！哇！馬戲團！」一個小女孩興奮地叫著。「媽媽，我想去看！可以嗎？」

「當然可以！」她的媽媽說。「還是免費的，眞好！」

每個人都既興奮又期待。馬戲團的經理在整理舞台，順便把那些馴服的動物們召喚過來。他用弓箭製作了一些空心的大圈圈，並用火球將之點燃。

「很好！」他笑著喃喃自語。「現在我們只需等到星期六了！」

四百英哩之外，在樂凡第和林特魁司的邊界處，克喜那群人正在休息，他們走了很遠的一段路了。他的蟲洞機器因爲當時從因努回到樂凡第的行程而故障了。

他們所在的這裡很平靜，只能聽到鳥叫的聲音。這時候有一個人從山丘另一頭出現，向著克喜他們跑過來。他有一雙很寬大的眼睛，戴著黑色的帽子，看起來像個普通的村漢。

「呵，呵，呵……」他正在喘氣。「你們有沒有聽說那個戰事？」

People were curios and started to come to look at the posters.

"Ooh! Ooh! Circus!" a little girl screamed excitedly. "Mommy, I want to see the show! Can we go?"

"Of course," said her mother. "It's FREE! How wonderful!"

Everybody got excited and was looking forward to it. As the manager of the circus was setting up the stage, he also summoned the tamed tigers, horses, and elephants. He made hoops out of arrows and lit them on fire with a fire ball.

"All good," he whispered and smiled. "Now we just have to wait 'till Saturday."

400 miles away, on the border of La Frontier and Lintercrest, Chrishie and his group were resting from a long trek. His wormhole machine broke down when they teleported from Yinu to La Frontier.

Everything was quiet and peaceful, they could only hear birds singing on the trees. A man appeared on a hill next to a village, running towards Chrishie's group. He had big wide eyes and was wearing a black hat, looking like a normal village man.

"Heh heh…," he was gasping. "Have you heard of the war?"

「什麼戰事?」真要昇關切地問。

那人述說強柯展開他的攻擊,而且快贏了。

「在芬溪那個跳越區,就是現在!」那人說。

「我們得去幫他們。」蝦肉說。

「是的,我們得去!」真要昇說,他轉向克喜。「這一定就是那最大的戰役!」

克喜思忖著。

「如果你們想幫忙,現在就要趕快出發,不然就太遲了!」那人說。

「OK!我們走吧!」克喜說。

「等一等!」可愛怡太太說。「我們可不可以先把布理布理帶回去可愛怡聖壇?」

「讓他自己決定吧!」克喜回答,看著布理布理。

「我想要跟他們一起戰鬥!」布理布理叫著。「我要跟克喜一起走!」

「好吧......」可愛怡太太嘆了口氣,答應了。

克喜他們掉頭,換了方向,前往芬溪。

他們離開很遠之後,那個村漢扯掉他的喬裝,露出一個又大又邪惡的微笑。

"What war?" TruEthan asked with great concerns.

The guy started to tell them about how Jrunk initiated an attack and was winning.

"This is happening at Fancì right now," said the person.

"We have to help them," said Sharo.

"Yes, we do," said TruEthan, turning to Chrishie. "This must be THE battle!"

Chrishie was thinking.

"If you want to help, you should go now before it is too late!" said the guy.

"Okay! Let's go then," said Chrishie.

"Wait!" said Mrs. Kawaii. "Can we bring Bri-Bri back to Kawaii Altar?"

"Let's see what he chooses," said Chrishie, looking at Bri-Bri.

"I want to FIGHT!" shouted Bri-Bri. "I want to go with Chrishie!"

"All right...," Mrs. Kawaii agreed with a sigh.

Chrishie and the group changed the direction and started to head to Fancì.

After Chrishie's group left, the village man tore off his disguise and showed a big and evil grin on his face.

第三十二章 # 大戰役（上）

　　星期六到了，馬戲團開始上演好戲。那個喬裝的村漢也來到可愛怡聖壇看馬戲團表演。

　　「好啊！」他喃喃自語。「非常好！」

　　在很遠的樂凡第南邊，與芬溪交界處，克喜那群人正在一個小餐館停下來用午餐。他們剛好看到電視上在播新聞。

　　「林特魁司馬戲團正在可愛怡聖壇做免費的精彩演出！怎麼有這麼好康的事？！除了跳火圈、老虎、蛇、等等，還有更多等你來觀賞！這都要感謝大方的馬戲團老闆，愛登先生！每個人都爭先恐後要進來看表演，現在這裡已有好幾千人！」記者正在報導。

　　螢幕上秀出一張馬戲團老闆愛登的照片。

　　「咦，你們不覺得他長的有點像阿努比斯嗎？」蝦肉盯著螢幕，邊看邊問。

Chapter XXXII The Great Battle Part I

On Saturday, the circus started to put on a show. The disguised village man also came to watch the circus show in Kawaii Altar.

"Good," he muttered, "very good."

Far away in the south of La Frontier, on the border to Fancì, Chrishie and his group was stopping by a diner for lunch. They happened to see a news on the TV.

"Lintercrest Circus is performing a FREE show at Kawaii Altar! How good is that? That have flaming hoops, tigers, snakes and many more! All this is brought to you by the generous circus owner and manager, Aiden. Everyone is rushing to the stadium tent. There are thousands and thousands of people here!" said the reporter.

A picture of the circus manager, Aiden, flashed on the screen.

"Well, don't you guys think he kind of looks like Anubis?" Sharo stared at the screen and asked.

「沒錯！這是阿努比斯！」布理布理大叫。畢竟他跟阿努比斯住在一起三年，所以對阿努比斯的長相很熟悉。

「他在那裡搞一個馬戲團幹什麼？」艾迪亞問。她們三個女孩子剛剛才吃了紫羅蘭花，所以有聲音可以說話。

「要賺錢？」潔兒猜。

「但這表演是免費的！」迷蝶說。

「是啊……等等！看啊！那個人不是我們昨天碰到的村漢嗎？」蝦肉指著螢幕，那個人正混在人群中。

「奇怪了，這是巧合嗎？」克喜覺得不解。

「啊！我們中計了！」將安大叫。

「什麼意思？中誰的計？」眞要昇問。大部分的人都還覺得很迷惑。

「芬溪根本就沒有戰事！這個人是要調虎離山，把我們引開，不去可愛怡聖壇。他一定是想在那裡搞什麼鬼！」將安用邏輯得到這樣的推論。

「那在可愛怡聖壇會發生什麼？他又爲什麼不想讓我們去那裡呢？」克喜問。

「強柯！我的天啊！他是強柯！」蝦肉尖叫起來。他一向對影像很有直覺，而且很能把線索連貫起來。「他以前就曾經用喬裝來騙過我們，記得嗎？這就是他！我們又被騙了！」

224

"Yes! That's Anubis!" Bri-Bri yelled. After all he had spent 3 years with Anubis, so he was very familiar with Anubis's look.

"What is he doing up there for a circus show?" asked Adiale. The girls had just ate one violet each so they could speak.

"Making more money?" guessed Jade.

"But the show is free!" said Misty.

"Right… Wait! See! Isn't that the village man we just met yesterday?" Sharo pointed to the screen. That guy was in the middle of crowd.

"Weird…. Is this a coincidence?" Chrishie was wondering.

"Ah! We've been tricked!" shouted John.

"What do you mean? Tricked by whom?" asked TruEthan. Most of them were still confused.

"There's no war in Fancì at all. That guy distracted us from going to Kawaii Altar because he was scheming something there," John figured this out using logic.

"But what will be happening in Kawaii Altar? And why didn't he want us to be there?" asked Chrishie.

"Jrunk! OMG! He is Jrunk!" screamed Sharo. He was always good in visions and connecting the dots. "He had tricked us before with his disguise, remember? That's him again!"

眾人都驚詫不已。

「那他是和阿努比斯合夥起來要搞鬼嗎？」艾迪亞激動地問。

「應該是。」可愛怡先生說。「我很擔心我在可愛怡聖壇的族人。」

眞要昇用手掌重重地拍自己的額頭，非常地懊惱。克喜腦中一片空白，不知該說什麼。

「現在怎麼辦？」阿米問。

「我們離可愛怡聖壇太遠了！要怎樣才能儘快趕到那裡呢？」艾迪亞問。

「我可以找一架私人噴射機帶我們很快地回去。」可愛怡太太說。

「好辦法！」克喜和眞要昇異口同聲地說。

於是他們去到最近的機場，可愛怡夫婦租了一架私人噴射機，他們就直接飛往可愛怡聖壇。

當他們抵達時，在馬戲團大帳棚的外面，黑暗正將可愛怡聖壇中央的天空籠罩住。強柯已經開始用掐息人的黑暗魔法殺人，人們到處逃竄尖叫。

「警察！逮捕這個人！」一個生意人大聲咆哮。

Everyone was shocked.

"Is he scheming something along with Anubis?" Adiale asked agitatedly.

"Looks like it," Mr. Kawaii said. "I'm worried about my clan people in Kawaii Altar."

TruEthan smacked his forehead, very upset. Chrishie was shocked and blank, not knowing what to say.

"Now what?" Armi asked.

"We are so far away from Kawaii Altar. How can we get there as soon as possible?" asked Adiale.

"I can find a private jet to get us back quickly," said Mrs. Kawaii.

"That sounds like a plan!" said Chrishie and TruEthan.

They went to the nearest airport. Mr. and Mrs. Kawaii rented a private jet and they flew to Kawaii Altar.

When they got there, outside the circus tent, the darkness was covering the sky of central Kawaii Altar. Jrunk had already started choking and killing people using the darkness. People were running and screaming everywhere.

"Police! Arrest this guy!" shouted a business man.

有一個女人很慌張地大喊：「史帝夫！你在哪裡？」

「救命啊！救命啊！這有在直播嗎？有沒有人可以來幫我們……」一個帶著孫女的老人大喊著。

「天啊！」一個五年級的男生害怕地叫著。「為什麼有個莫名其妙跑出來的人在隨機殺人呢？」他開始左右張望，想看看有沒有哪裡有出口可以逃出去。在他旁邊一個年紀較大的男孩說：

「我已經找過了，到處都被鐵柵欄圍起來。」

黑暗抓住人們，讓他們慢慢窒息而死，一個接著一個。

那個老先生跌倒了。

「爺爺！爺爺！快起來！不然我們都會被殺死！」他的孫女哭喊著，無助地坐在地上。

當克喜他們到了那裡，看到這一場混亂的景象，就知道他們得馬上做些什麼，不然就太遲了。

阿米拿出他的超級手電筒，因為他知道它的強光可以驅走黑暗。但是它竟然不管用，沒有光線出來。

「不會吧？！」阿米喊著，「沒有電了！」

「艾迪亞！你是可愛怡家族的拯救者！」可愛怡先生對著艾迪亞大叫，試著蓋過那些吵雜的聲音和混亂。

A woman was panicking and crying out, "Steve! Where are you?"

"Help! Help! Is this a broadcast? If you can reach us... HELP!" shouted an old man with his granddaughter.

"OH MY GOD!!" shouted a fifth grader, in horror. "Why does this random guy want to kill us all?" He started to look around to see if there were any escape routes. An older boy next to him said,

"I checked all the routes, it is surrounded by metal bars."

The darkness grabbed people, chocking them slowly, one by one. Then they would die in a few minutes.

The old man got tripped. "Grandpa! Grandpa! Get up! We'll die!" cried the granddaughter, sitting on the ground, hopelessly.

Once they arrived and saw this chaos, Chrishie and his group knew that they needed to do something immediately or it would be too late.

Armi took out his super flashlight because he knew it could stop the darkness. However, it didn't work. There was no light.

"Oh no!" cried Armi. "It's out of battery!"

"Adiale! You are the savior of Kawaii family!" Mr. Kawaii shouted to her, trying to overcome the loud noise and mess.

艾迪亞拿出她在雷電市集買的霹靂閃電，向強柯的方向丟過去。它發出嚇人的轟隆隆的雷聲及閃電，強柯因此分心了一下，但並沒有任何影響。

此時，在她身邊的老人戴天尼提醒她可以用他之前教她的爾卓式。艾迪亞有好一陣子沒有使用法力了，她試著回想，然後要開始操作手勢。但老人戴天尼阻止了她，說：

「爾卓式是用來取消或刪除跳越區的，如果你單單使用爾卓式，它將會摧毀現在在可愛怡聖壇的每一個人。」

「那我該怎麼辦？」艾迪亞問。

「我之前教真要昇的那招『靈魂之風』是一種愛和保護的法力，它可以和爾卓式一起被使用，來平衡其法力，這樣就可以只摧毀特定的目標。」

於是真要昇就開始操作「靈魂之風」的手勢。那股風流進艾迪亞的爾卓式，形成了一個球狀，能量從裂縫中流洩出來。

就在這時候，阿努比斯發現了克喜他們來攪局，非常不爽。他朝他們發射弓箭，他們忙著閃躲。克喜在等著艾迪亞用爾卓式的法力，沒注意到有一枝箭正向他射來。

Adiale took out the thunderbolt that she bought from the Thunder Market. She threw it towards Jrunk, which made a terrifying thunderous sound and flashes of lightening. It distracted Jrunk for a moment, but it did not do any harm to him.

Derteinium, who was right next to her, reminded her about Adro that he taught her. Adiale had not used the power for a long time. She tried her best to recall, then started to do the movement of Adro. However, Derteinium stopped her, saying,

"Adro is used to undo and delete Jumpers. If you use Adro by itself, it will kill everyone in Kawaii Altar."

"Then what can I do?" asked Adiale.

"The Wind of the Soul that I taught TruEthan is a power of love and protection. It can be used together with Adro to balance the destroying power, and only damage the specific targets."

Then TruEthan started doing the movement for the Wind of the Soul. The wind summoned by TruEthan flew into the Adro power by Adiale. They formed an orb crackled with energy.

At the same time, Anubis was very unhappy finding Chrishie's group was here disturbing his plan. He fired arrows at them. They were busy dodging the arrows. Chrishie was distracted anticipating the Adro to happen, he did not notice that an arrow was coming his way.

「不！！」眞要昇大叫。

他俯衝過去，把克喜推開。那枝箭射進眞要昇的的胸膛，鮮血湧出來，濺到地上，像一條紅色的小溪。

"Nooooo!!!" shouted TruEthan.

He dived in to block the arrow, pushing Chrishie away. The arrow hit TruEthan's chest. He fell down. Blood sprang and spilled on the ground, like a stream in red.

第三十三章 # 大戰役（下）

「真要昇！不！」克喜大叫。

「我可以用我的鬼魂法力來醫治他。」若薇亞公主說。「可是可能需要很久的時間。」

「拜託妳了！」克喜焦急地說。

布理布理覺得他必須去阻止阿努比斯，不然他的朋友們都會死在阿努比斯的箭下。所以他就跳到阿努比斯的面前。

「蘋果，蘋果，跳個曼波！」他一邊叫，一邊對著阿努比斯搖屁股。然後又轉過身來，繼續搖屁股。

「蘋果，蘋果，跳個曼波！」

阿努比斯朝布理布理射了一箭。

「閃到左邊！」卡爾王子喊著。他是個經驗豐富的弓箭手，所以知道如何躲避。

「哈哈！沒中！你太遜了！」布理布理繼續搗亂。「蘋果，蘋果，跳個曼波！」

Chapter XXXIII The Great Battle Part II

"TruEthan! No!" shouted Chrishie.

"I can heal him with my ghost powers," Princess Rovia said. "But it might take a while to heal."

"Please!" said Chrishie.

Bri-Bri felt that he needed to stop Anubis from firing arrows, or his friends would all be killed by Anubis. So Bri-Bri jumped over in front of Anubis.

"Apple! Apple! Dance and ripple!" shouted Bri-Bri, while shaking his butt at Anubis. He twirled around and started shaking his butt again.

"Apple! Apple! Dance and ripple!"

Anubis threw an arrow at Bri-Bri.

"Dodge to the left!" shouted Prince Kale. He was an experienced archer, so he knew which way to go when an arrow comes at you.

"Ha! Ha! You missed! You suck at this!" Bri-Bri continued. "Apple! Apple! Dance and ripple!"

阿努比斯停下來，咆哮說：

「閉嘴！你煩死了！」

艾迪亞終於發射出爾卓式，一道強光照亮了每個人的眼前。阿努比斯即時溜掉，來到潔兒的身後。迷蝶看到了，心想要警告她妹妹潔兒，於是趕緊跑向克喜的背包那裡，想要吃掉最後一朵紫羅蘭花。匆忙中她不小心被克喜的背包絆倒了，一個東西從背包中滾出來，是克喜在雷電市集買的那個改變聲音的機器。花盆剛好壓到機器的「啟動」鍵。

迷蝶站起來，一邊吞下紫羅蘭花，一邊用眼睛搜尋她的妹妹潔兒，想確認她的安全，但是她並沒有看到潔兒。於是迷蝶大喊：

「你在哪裡？」她的聲音顯然因為那個機器的關係被改變了。

聽到這個聲音，強柯整個人僵住，突然停止他殺人的舉動。

Anubis stopped and yelled, "SHUT UP!!! It's so annoying!"

Adiale finally let go of the Adro, a flash of bright light shined in front of everyone. Anubis slipped away in time and came behind Jade, who was helping the Kawaii people to escape. Misty saw this and tried to warn Jade. Misty ran over to Chrishie's backpack, looking for the last violet to swallow. She tripped over Chrishie's backpack in haste. Something got knocked out, it's the voice-changing machine from the Thunder Market. The flower pot landed on the activation button of the machine.

Misty stood up, swallowing the violet and trying to make sure Jade was safe. But she did not see Jade in her sight. She cried out,

"Where are you?" Apparently her voice was changed because of the machine.

Jrunk was frozen and suddenly stopped his action of killing, upon hearing this voice.

「羅蘭……是妳嗎？」強柯喃喃說著。「是妳嗎？羅蘭？」

艾迪亞射出的電漿擊倒了強柯，使他跌跪在地上，並且失去所有的法力。

蝦肉和將安見機衝過來，在強柯的兩側，用盡最大的力氣抓住他，讓他動彈不得。這時，有個東西從強柯的口袋中掉出來，是他在翠尼提展場玩遊戲得來的絨毛蜥蜴娃娃。蝦肉看到這個，想起了他們在樂凡第一起出遊的情景，以及那一天的友誼。

「你為什麼要當一個壞蛋呢？」蝦肉嘆了一口氣，輕聲地說。「你為什麼要殺這些無辜的人呢？你可以成為一個好人，一個很好的朋友的。」

「我很憤怒……因為失去了羅蘭。」強柯回答。

「羅蘭正在看著你。」蝦肉說。「她如果知道你變成這樣的人，一定不會高興的。」

「如果羅蘭變成一個邪惡的人，你會高興嗎？」將安問。

「不！她是世界上心地最善良的人！」

「那就對啦！」將安說。「所以你應該作個好人。」

「為了羅蘭的緣故。」蝦肉補充。

「而且你也可以交到許多好朋友，會更快樂!」 將安說。

"Violet…, is that you?" murmured Jrunk. "Is that you? Violet?"

The plasma from Adiale's Adro power struck Jrunk and made him fall on his knees, losing all his power.

Sharo and John dashed to Jrunk's sides and grabbed his hands with all their might, making sure he couldn't move. Then, something fell out of Jrunk's pocket. It was the stuffed lizard that he won at Trinity fair. Sharo remembered about the friendship they had with Jrunk when they gave the tour in La Frontier.

"Why do you have to be a villain?" Sharo sighed and asked softly. "Why do you want to kill these innocent people? You would make a good person and a good friend."

"I was angry… because of losing Violet," answered Jrunk.

"Violet is watching over you," said Sharo. "She would not be proud of you for who you became."

"Would you like it if Violet became evil?" asked John.

"No! She was the kindest person in the world!"

"There you go!" said John. "So you'd better be a good person."

"For Violet's sake," added Sharo.

"You can also make friends and be happy!" said John.

　　強柯想起當時眞要昇和布理布理邀請他一起去樂凡第玩，那天跟著他們一起，眞的很有趣。當初他到底爲什麼會變成壞人的呢？他因爲羅蘭的死而想要報復，但是那並不是任何人的錯，不是嗎？那是他們自己造成的。所以，爲了什麼？看看這些被自己殺死的人們，這一切到底是爲了什麼？

　　「我不知道爲什麼……」強柯喃喃說著，非常地迷茫。然後他抬頭看到迷蝶。

　　「妳的聲音和羅蘭的一樣。」他對她說。

　　「呃……那是個意外。」迷蝶回答，笑得有點尷尬。

　　「那聲音也很適合妳的笑容，非常甜美和溫暖。」強柯說。「讓我想起羅蘭。」

　　迷蝶臉紅了起來。

　　就在同時，卡爾王子把潔兒從阿努比斯的手中救出來。阿努比斯已經逃得不知去向了。

Jrunk remembered the time when TruEthan and Bri-Bri kindly offered him the tour of La Frontier. It was really fun, traveling with friends. Why had he ever wanted to become evil? He wanted revenge for Violet's death, but it was nobody's fault but themselves', wasn't it? So, why? Looking at all these people killed by him, what's this all about?

"I don't know why I turned evil," Jrunk murmured, feeling very lost. Then he looked up at Misty.

"You have Violet's voice," he said to her.

"Um.., it must have been an accident," said Misty, smiling a bit awkwardly.

"It suits your smile, very warm and sweet," said Jrunk. "It also reminds me of Violet." Misty blushed.

In the meantime, Prince Kale managed to rescue Jade form Anubis, who had fled to nowhere.

第三十四章 # 真相揭曉

　　現在戰役結束了，一切都逐漸恢復平靜。可愛怡聖壇的人們不是忙著把受傷的人送往醫院，就是在互相幫忙尋找走失的親人、朋友。

　　當若薇亞公主正在為眞要昇療傷時，每個人也因長時間的作戰而精疲力竭。這時候，克喜突然召聚大家，神情嚴肅，很不尋常。他說：

　　「在佛夢達經歷過這些之後，我想現在該是我告訴你們一些事的時候了。」

　　「一些事是什麼事？」布理布理好奇地問。

　　「這一切都要從安卓‧藍普提開始說起。他是老人戴天尼的姪子。」克喜說。「他在 1999 年時寫了一個演算法，叫做『大十』。但是他在 2015 年時死於一場車禍意外。」

　　「你為什麼要告訴我們這個？」強柯問。

　　「因為他要你們知道關於佛夢達的眞相。」眞要昇說。

Chapter XXXIV The Truth Revealed

Now the battle was over, things had quietened down. The people of Kawaii Altar were either rushing to send injured people to hospitals, or helping each other looking for their families or friends.

While Princess Rovia was curing TruEthan from Anubis's arrow, and everyone was exhausted from fighting for the whole day, Chrishie called the group over, being unusually serious. He said,

"After all we have been through in Formonda, I guess it's time for me to tell you *something*."

"What's *something*?" Bri-Bri was curious.

"It all started with Andrew Lamputi. He was Derteinium's nephew," Chrishie said. "He wrote an algorithm called Dash in 1999. But he died in a car accident in 2015."

"Why are you telling us this?" asked Jrunk.

"Because he wants you to know the truth of Formonda," said TruEthan.

「安卓有一個遠見，要用大十演算法來創造虛擬世界。我 12 歲那年在網路上認識他，那時候我已經開始學習寫程式，而且也很喜歡打電動遊戲。他問我有沒有興趣來學大十，我說好啊，他就把所有的東西都教我。很快地，我就用大十創造出佛夢達。」

「啊！我記得第一次碰到你的時候，你曾經告訴過我大十魔法。」艾迪亞說。

「是的，它其實是一種電動遊戲的演算法。我和我的好朋友，真要昇和阿米，常常在一起玩這個遊戲。我們想到用另一種語言來命名我所創造的這個世界，就決定叫它『佛夢達』，它的意思是『夢裡的探險』。」

「所以，你是說……」迷蝶說，「我們不是真實存在的？」

「這……我們，包括所有在佛夢達裡面的人，都只是虛擬的？」卡爾王子問。

「等一等！」布理布理叫說，「我是個假的？」

「呃……可以這樣說……」克喜回答。

所有的人，尤其是佛夢達裡面的人，都太過震驚而說不出話來。

「我們三個人都有貢獻，不是只有克喜一個人。」真要昇說。「比如說，愛的運動那個跳越區就是我造的，但是後來被強柯佔領了，改成強柯運動。」

"Andrew had the vision of using Dash to create virtual worlds. I met him on the Internet when I was 12, at that time I had started coding and was very into video games. He asked me if I'd be interested in coding Dash. I said yes. So he taught me everything. Soon, I created this world Formonda using Dash."

"Yeah, I remember you told me about Dash when I first met you," said Adiale.

"Yes, it actually was an algorithm for video games. My best friends, TruEthan and Armi, and I played them a lot together. We thought of using a name that means 'adventure in a dream' in a different language, and decided to use Formonda as the name for this world I created."

"So, you're telling us…," said Misty, "we are not *real*?"

"Um… we, including everyone who came from Formonda, are just *virtual reality*?" asked Prince Kale.

"Wait — " shouted Bri-Bri, "I AM FAKE???"

"Well, in a way, yes…," said Chrishie.

People, mainly those from Formonda, were all shocked and speechless.

"All three of us contributed, not just Chrishie," said TruEthan. "For example, I created the Jumper of Love

Movement, which got taken over by Jrunk later and changed to Jrunk Movement."

「我造了追夢麗、富可寧、和芬溪。」阿米說。

「我還造了博列姆和可愛怡聖壇!」真要昇說。

「而我,」克喜說,「我造了阿努比斯之臉,勁剋司,波理斯瑪,樂凡第,還有其他許多地方,包括雷電市集。」

「所以你們知道佛夢達裡所有的事情囉?」可愛怡先生問。

「嗯,也不算是。我們只是創造,但是他們會自行演化。比如說我們就不知道傳瑞德後來會變成強柯,變成一個大壞蛋。」克喜說。

「那是在羅蘭死了之後……」強柯咕噥地說。

「是的,那也就是為什麼我很想知道佛夢達後來到底發生過些什麼事,因此我才想買那本歷史書。」真要昇說。

「等等!」潔兒說,「我有一個問題!你們這些從滴,底,球……你們是怎麼說的?」

「地球。」將安說。

「你們是怎麼進來佛夢達裡面的?」潔兒把話說完。

「這個問題應該要由老人戴天尼來回答。」克喜說。他轉向戴天尼,每一個人也都轉過去看他。於是老人戴天尼回答:

"I made the Jumpers Dreamryl, Frecenìn, and Fancī," said Armi.

"I also made Blem, and Kawaii Altar!" said TruEthan.

"And *I*," said Chrishie, "was the one who made the Face of Anubis, Zinx, Purisima, and La Frontier, and all the other stuff, including Thunder Market."

"So you guys know everything about Formonda?" asked Mr. Kawaii.

"Well, not really. We created them, but they evolved by themselves. For instance, we did not know that Fred would turn to Jrunk and become a villain," Chrishie said.

"That's after Violet died…," Jrunk murmured.

"Right. That's why I was so eager to learn what had happened in Formonda and wanted to get the history book," said TruEthan.

"Wait!" said Jade, "I have a question. How did the people from Errth, E-R-th, however you say it — "

"Earth," said John.

"How did you get into Formonda?" Jade finished her sentence.

"Derteinium is the best person to answer this question," said Chrishie, turning to Derteinium. So Derteinium answered,

「嗯……我發明了一個機器，可以藉由實物的幻象把人們帶進虛擬的世界。它讓人們可以在真實及虛擬的世界中來回穿梭，我把它叫做『邀請通道』。安卓弄出一個密碼，就是 Who-You-You-Who，他把這密碼放進他的程式裡面，所以邀請通道只能被這個密碼啟動。」

「啊！原來如此……」現在艾迪亞比較明白了。

「我們想要測試一下這個機器。」老人戴天尼看著蝦肉和將安，說，「那就是為什麼安卓找到你們兩個。」

「邀請通道有一個功能，可以分別選擇要穿梭的真實世界和虛擬世界的時間點。安卓去到 1956 年和 1972 年，用 Who-You-You-Who 的密碼把你們兩個帶到了佛夢達來。當然，他並沒有跟著一起來，因為那時候他的演算法只能讓小孩子進入用大十寫成的虛擬世界。」

「後來我和老人戴天尼把這部分改掉了，所以現在無論是大人還是小孩都能來到佛夢達。」克喜補充。

「安卓和我還一起發明了蟲洞機器。他把它送給克喜當成一個禮物，那是在他還沒發生意外之前。」老人戴天尼說。

「安卓死的時候我非常傷心。」克喜說。「他是一個絕頂聰明的人，但是我只跟他學了一年的時間……」

"Well, I invented a machine that used the illusions of reality to bring people into the virtual world. It makes people able to travel between the real world and the virtual world. I called it 'Invite Tunnel'. Andrew created the passcode 'Who-You-You-Who' and put this in the algorithm. So the Invite Tunnel can only be activated by Who-You-You-Who."

"Ah, that's why…," now Adiale could put things together.

"We decided to try it out first," Derteinium then looked at Sharo and John. "That's why Andrew found you two."

"The Invite Tunnel has the feature for us to pick the specific time in the real world and in the virtual world to travel. Andrew went to 1956 and 1972, and tried with Who-You-You-Who to bring you two to Formonda. Of course he didn't come in with you. At that time the algorithm was written so only children could enter the virtual world written with Dash."

"Later, Derteinium and I changed it. So now anyone, kids or adults, can enter Formonda," Chrishie added.

"Andrew and I also invented the wormhole machine, which was given to Chrishie as a gift, just before Andrew died," Derteinium said.

"I was very, very sad when Andrew got killed in the accident," said Chrishie. "He was a super smart guy. But I only got to learn from him for a year…."

他繼續說，「然後我就找真要昇和阿米，請他們跟我一起來佛夢達。我們在這裡遇見了蝦肉和將安，一起旅行了一陣子。因為太多變化了，即使我自己也需要在這裡多探索一下。」

「然後，當我們碰到妳，」克喜轉向艾迪亞，「我就知道老人戴天尼已經完成他的使命了。」

「什麼使命？」艾迪亞問。

「老人戴天尼一直跟我說他必須回到過去，帶一個很特別的人來到佛夢達，雖然他怎麼也不肯告訴我那個人是誰，還有為什麼。當我看到妳時，我就知道妳就是他一直在說的那個人。」

「所以那個特別的人就是可愛怡家族的拯救者！」可愛怡太太說。

「我想是的。安卓在他的演算法裡放進一些連我都不知道的東西，比如說可愛怡家族的拯救者這件事我就不知道，我沒有寫這部分。」

「我在參觀『顯赫博物館』時就得到這個線索了！」蝦肉說。「這個資訊竟然被隱藏地保存下來，成為佛夢達的一個傳說。」

「所以你是說，你並不知道我為什麼會是可愛怡家族的拯救者？」艾迪亞問。

He continued, "Then I asked TruEthan and Armi to come with me to this world. We met Sharo and John when we first came here and we all traveled together for a while. Because of so many changes, even I needed to explore Formonda a bit more myself."

"Then, when we met you," Chrishie turned to Adiale, "I knew that Derteinium had completed his mission."

"What mission?" asked Adiale.

"Derteinium always told me that he had to go back in time to get someone special into Formonda, though he wouldn't tell me who and why. When I saw you, I knew you were the person Derteinium was talking about."

"So that special person was the savior of the Kawaii family!" Mrs. Kawaii said.

"I guess so. Andrew inserted some things in his algorithm that I might not know about. For example, the savior of Kawaii, I did not program that in my code."

"I got this clue from visiting the Grand Museum," said Sharo. "Somehow this piece of information had been hidden and kept as a legend in the history of Formonda."

"So, you mean that you do not know why *I am* the savior of Kawaii?" asked Adiale.

「我真的不知道。」克喜說。「也許安卓想要在每一個虛擬世界裡都有一個拯救者？」

「我在佛夢達這裡教你們的那些法力招式，都是本來遊戲中的指令。」老人戴天尼說。「比如說，爾卓式，最具有摧毀力的一個，就是刪除指令，它會把整個跳越區消除掉。」

「我也有一個問題。」強柯說。「為什麼羅蘭死了沒有化成鬼魂，然而在這裡的若薇亞小姐卻可以？」他指著若薇亞公主。

「哎——」克喜看起來有點不高興。「這都是真要昇的錯。是的，這完全是一個錯誤！若薇亞公主的命運是要死在波理斯瑪的那場大火的，但是真要昇救了她，因此打破了我當初程式裡寫的法則。原本在佛夢達裡面的人死了是不會化成鬼魂的，那也是一個寫好的法則。因為真要昇的破壞舉動，若薇亞公主變成是唯一的例外。」

克喜轉向真要昇說，「那是她的命運，我已經告訴過你了！真要昇，她應該是要死在波理斯瑪的！」

「我知道。」真要昇說。「對不起，克喜。但是即使再給我一次機會，我還是會做同樣的事。」

「我必須要謝謝你救了我妹妹，真要昇。」卡爾王子對他說。

"I personally don't know," replied Chrishie. "Maybe Andrew wanted to have a savior in every world?"

"Those powers that I teach you here in Formonda are actually commands in the game," Derteinium said. "For example, Adro, the most destructive one, is the delete command to remove an entire Jumper."

"I have a question, too," said Jrunk. "Why did Violet die without turning into a ghost but Miss Rovia did?" pointing to Princess Rovia.

"Well," said Chrishie, looking a bit annoyed, "It was all TruEthan's fault. Yes, *fault!* Princess Rovia's destiny was to die in the great fire of Purisima. But when TruEthan rescued her, he broke one of the laws in my code. Originally when a person in Formonda dies, there's no ghost. That's another law. Princess Rovia was the only exception because of the breach."

Chrishie turned to TruEthan and continued, "It was her destiny. I've told you, TruEthan. She was supposed to die there in Purisima!"

"I know," said TruEthan. "I'm sorry, Chrishie. But I would still do the same even if I had the chance again."

"I have to thank you, TruEthan, for saving my sister," said Prince Kale.

「這樣的話，我就什麼都不是——既不屬於佛夢達，也不屬於地球。那我到底是什麼？」若薇亞公主輕聲地、鎮靜地說。「我想我應該要去完成我的命運。」

「不可以！」眞要昇喊著。「千萬不可以！那樣我就再也見不到妳了！」

卡爾王子也很傷心。「妳非得要這樣做嗎？」他問她。

「每個故事都有完結的時候，每個故事也都會有失落的部分。」克喜說，瞥了強柯一眼。強柯眼裡流露著傷心，他現在終於確定他永遠也不可能再看到羅蘭了！

過了幾天，強柯跟迷蝶求婚，他們有一個很棒的婚禮。卡爾王子邀請潔兒跟他一起去旅行，潔兒很高興地答應了，因爲她也很想去到處看看，尤其又是有卡爾王子的陪伴。至於布理布理和他的家人，他們回到可愛怡聖壇，回到他們正常的生活。

「現在是時候回到波理斯瑪了！」若薇亞公主說。「我必須去完成我的命運。」

他們帶著若薇亞公主回去波理斯瑪，眞要昇和卡爾王子都哭了。克喜把手放在眞要昇的肩膀上，嘆了一口氣。

「不要！若薇亞！拜託妳！不要！」眞要昇的心都碎了。

"If that's the case, it means I'm nothing — not a part of Formonda, not a part of Earth. Then what am I?" Princess Rovia said very gently and calmly. "I think I need to fulfill my destiny."

"No!" cried TruEthan. "You can't! I won't be able to see you again!"

Prince Kale was sad, too. "Do you really have to?" he asked.

"Every story must come to an end. And every story must have some loss," said Chrishie. He cast a glance at Jrunk, who had sadness in his eyes. Now Jrunk was sure that he would never see Violet again.

After a few days, Jrunk proposed to Misty. They had a wonderful wedding. Prince Kale invited Jade to go traveling with him. Jade agreed happily because she loved to look around all the different Jumpers, especially with the company of Prince Kale. As for Bri-Bri and his parents, they went back to Kawaii Altar and returned to their normal life.

"Now it's time for me to return to Purisima," said Princess Rovia. "I must go back to fulfill my destiny."

They brought Princess Rovia to Purisima. Both TruEthan and Prince Kale started to cry. Chrishie put his hand on TruEthan's shoulder and sighed.

"No! Rovia! Please, no!" TruEthan was heartbroken.

「我會永遠愛你，親愛的眞要昇。」若薇亞公主說。「還記得我寫給你的那首詩嗎？它表達了所有我對你的愛。我很高興能有機會遇見你，還跟你一起去冒險。那是我一生中最棒的時光！」

　　「現在是說再見的時候了……」若薇亞公主跨過了邊界。

　　「若薇亞！」眞要昇哭喊著，他的手伸出去，想要最後一次觸摸她那若隱似現的手。

　　她的藍色頭髮漸漸地淡去，她的身體也是。然後，她整個人完全消逝不見了。

　　眞要昇倒在地上啜泣不已，許久，許久。

"I will love you forever, my dear TruEthan," said Princess Rovia. "Remember that poem? It expressed all my love to you. I'm glad I had the chance to meet you and adventure with you. It was the best time in my life!"

"Now it's time to say good-bye…," Princess Rovia crossed the border.

"Rovia!" cried TruEthan as he reached out to touch Princess Rovia's misty hands one last time.

Her blue hair started to fade, so did her whole body. Then, she disappeared, completely.

TruEthan fell on the ground and sobbed for a long, long time.

尾聲 1975 年，世界博覽會

　　Aquapolis 是在日本沖繩島海邊的一個人工海上浮城。這個建築物的一部分是沉浸在水面下的，像個潛水艇一樣。它獨自站在水中，看起來就像一個巨大的方形船艦。

　　這是 1975 年的世界博覽會，將安和他的爸媽一起來這裡過暑假。他正急忙要趕去 Aquapolis，它是這個展覽中一個吸睛的景點。在路上他不小心撞到一個人。

　　「唉唷！」那個男人叫道。

　　「對不起。」將安說。

　　那個男人揉著肩膀，看了將安一眼。

　　「嘿！」他突然變得很興奮。「將安！」

　　「蛤？你怎麼會知道我的名字？」將安問。

　　這個男人大約三十幾歲，黑頭髮，膚色有點蒼白，眼睛閃著亮光，看起來很聰明。

Epilogue **EXPO 1975**

Aquapolis was an artificial floating city on the coast of Okinawa island in Japan. Part of its structure was immersed underwater, like a submarine. It looked like a gigantic square ship standing in the water by itself.

This was the World's Fair of 1975. John came here with his parents for a summer vacation. As he was rushing to the Aquapolis, one of the main attractions for this exhibition, he bumped into a man.

"Ouch!" said the man.

"Sorry," said John.

The man was rubbing his shoulder, then he looked at John.

"Hey!" the man suddenly became excited. "John!"

"Huh? How do you know my name?" asked John.

This man probably was in his mid-30's. He had black hair and pale skin. His eyes were sparkling, looked pretty neat and smart.

「啊！我猜你認不出我來。」那個人說。「我是蝦肉。記得嗎？佛夢達！」

「蝦肉？」將安問。「你是蝦肉？」將安現在十八歲，這是他從佛夢達回來的三年後。

「是啊！」蝦肉笑著。「我知道我現在看起來不太一樣，我是個大人了。」

看著一個已經長成大人的蝦肉，並且和他說話，將安的確覺得怪怪的。畢竟在佛夢達一起歷險的時候，他們是一樣的年紀和身高。

「能在這麼久之後看到你真是太棒了！」蝦肉一邊說一邊給他一個大擁抱。

「嗯，對我來說，只有三年而已……」將安喃喃地說。

「我記得你和你表哥住在德國，不是嗎？」將安問。

「是，但我在 25 歲那年回日本來工作。」

蝦肉繼續說，「我們去找點食物來吃吧！我想試試美國食物。」

「Yeah! 你會很喜歡的！」將安說。「有漢堡、雞塊、奶昔，還有薯條……」

"Ah, I guess you cannot recognize me," said the man. "I'm Sharo. Remember? Formonda!"

"Sharo?" asked John. "You're Sharo?" John was 18 now, three years after he went to Formonda.

"Yes!" Sharo was smiling. "I know I've looked different. I'm a grown-up now."

John did feel a bit weird seeing and talking to a grown-up Sharo. They used to be at the same age and height when they adventured together in Formonda.

"It's so good to see you again after so long!" said Sharo, giving him a big hug.

"Um… only three years, at least for me…," murmured John.

"I remember you lived in Germany with your cousin?" asked John.

"Ya, but I moved back to Japan for work when I was 25."

Sharo continued, "Let's go get some food. I want to try some American food."

"Yeah, you'll love it!" said John. "There are hamburgers, chicken nuggets, milk shakes, and French fries…."

「薯條？」蝦肉問。「那不是法國食物嗎？」（註：薯條的英文原意是「法式油炸物」。）

「喔，我也不知道。」將安聳聳肩說。「是叫做法式，但我想其實應該是美國食物。」

當他們嘴裡塞滿了食物，正在邊吃邊看展覽時，將安又撞到了一個女人。

「嘿！小伙子！拜託你走路看路！你差一點打翻我的食物！」那個女人對他很大聲地說。

「對不起，我不是故意的。」將安說。「但是妳不該在公共場所對別人大吼大叫。」

「什麼？多管閒事的小子！」她很生氣。

「聽起來好耳熟。」蝦肉自言自語，開始打量那個女人。她大概五十幾歲，臉上有雀斑，一頭短髮。

「嗯……艾迪亞？」蝦肉認人的功夫還是很厲害。

「什麼？艾，艾迪，艾迪亞？！」將安的下巴掉下來，嘴裡的食物差點掉出來。

那個女人剛開始看著蝦肉，一臉困惑。然後她轉頭仔細看著將安，她臉上的表情立即大變。

「將安！啊！啊！啊！我的天啊！」

"French fries?" asked Sharo. "So they are French food?"

"Well, I don't know," John shrugged. "They're called French but I think they are actually American food."

While they were stuffing their mouths full and looking through the exhibits on display, John, again, bumped into a woman.

"Hey youngster! You'd better watch where you're going! You almost knocked over my food!" yelled that woman.

"Sorry, I didn't mean to do that," said John. "Still though, you shouldn't yell at people in public."

"What? You should mind your own business, kid!" she was upset.

"This sounds so familiar," murmured Sharo, paying attention to that woman. She was in her 50's, with freckles on her face and short hair.

"Um… Adiale?" Sharo was still very good in recognizing people's faces.

"What?! Ad-Adia-Adiale?" John's jaw dropped and the food almost fell out of his open mouth.

The lady was perplexed at first looking at Sharo. Then, when she looked at John more carefully, her facial expression changed instantly.

"John?! Oh! Oh! Oh! My! God!"

自從他們在佛夢達最後一次見面，艾迪亞的外表顯然有了很大的變化。

「還有蝦肉！哇！我沒想到會在這裡碰到你們！」艾迪亞用高頻的尖聲叫著。

將安用手塞住他的耳朵，說：「真的是艾迪亞沒錯。」

就在這時候，一個有著金黃色捲髮的小孩子，大約三歲左右，向他們跑過來，不小心跌倒了。

「外婆！外婆！我想去水裡玩！」那個小男孩喊著。

「好，好，好！我的小寶貝！」艾迪亞把他抱起來，在他臉頰上親了一下。然後她轉向將安和蝦肉，說：

「來見見我的外孫，他叫安卓·藍普提。」

Adiale's appearance surely had changed a lot from the last time they met in Formonda.

"And Sharo! Wow! I didn't think I'd meet any of you here!" shouted Adiale, with her high-pitched voice.

John covered his ears with hands, and said, "Yeah, you are truly Adiale."

Right at this moment, a small child with curly blonde hair, about 3 years old, ran towards them and stumbled.

"Grandma! Grandma! I want to go play in the water!" cried out the little boy.

"Okay, okay, my sweetie!" Adiale picked him up and gave him a kiss on his cheek. Then she turned to John and Sharo, and said,

"I want you to meet him, my grandson, Andrew Lamputi."

佛夢達系列

第一集：可愛怡家族的命運

國家圖書館出版品預行編目資料

佛夢達：可愛怡家族的命運／王克謙、王凱琳合
著. —初版.—臺中市：白象文化，2018.1
　　　面：　公分.——
　　ISBN 978-986-358-580-0(平裝)

859.6　　　　　　　　　　106021018

佛夢達：可愛怡家族的命運

作　　　者　王克謙、王凱琳

譯　　　者　王凱琳

校　　　對　王凱琳

專案主編　林孟侃

出版經紀　徐錦淳、林榮威、吳適意、林孟侃、陳逸儒

設計創意　張禮南、何佳諠

經銷推廣　李莉吟、莊博亞、劉育姍、李如玉

營運管理　張輝潭、林金郎、黃姿虹、黃麗穎、曾千熏

發 行 人　張輝潭

出版發行　白象文化事業有限公司

　　　　　402台中市南區美村路二段392號

　　　　　出版、購書專線：（04）2265-2939

　　　　　傳真：（04）2265-1171

印　　　刷　普羅文化股份有限公司

初版一刷　2018 年 1 月

　　二刷　2018 年 2 月

　　三刷　2019 年 9 月

定　　　價　395 元